10690602

Hillbilly Hollow
& Rapture Grange

First Edition

Published by The Nazca Plains Corporation
Las Vegas, Nevada
2011

ISBN: 978-1-61098-173-6
E-Book: 978-161098-174-3

Published by

The Nazca Plains Corporation ®
4640 Paradise Rd, Suite 141
Las Vegas NV 89109-8000

PUBLISHER'S NOTE
Hillbilly Hollow & Rapture Grange is a work of fiction created
wholly by *Bob Archman's* imagination. All characters are fictional
and any resemblance to any persons living or deceased is purely by
accident. No portion of this book reflects any real person or events.

Cover,
Art Director, Blake Stephens

DEDICATION

Hillbilly Hollow
& Rapture Grange

First Edition

Bob Archman

CONTENTS

PART ONE: IN THE HOLLOW

Contents Continued...

PART TWO: RAPTURE GRANGE

PART ONE: IN THE HOLLOW

Chapter 1

My Dad said Hillbilly Hollow was a place that stretched from Nowhere to East Nowhere. It was a secluded valley in Virginia's Blue Ridge and out of the way even by the standards of Mountain Virginia. Only one road served it. It was six twisting and turning miles from my hometown, Marshall City, Virginia. Marshall City wasn't exactly the most sophisticated place in Virginia, but we always considered ourselves to be downright city slickers compared to the inhabitants of Hillbilly Hollow.

The residents of the Hollow were either Wilsons, Clancies or their kin. Dad said they had been there since Noah and they stayed to themselves. Everyone knew they lived in the hollow, married in the hollow and eventually died there. The marrying part got them in trouble. Way too many cousins married other cousins and Mom said they just about made a new species. Mom was the science teacher in the High School. Dad was the minister of the Presbyterian Church.

I knew them well because Ronnie Wilson was my best friend. We met when we were in kindergarten. We remained friends through high school. Ronnie would stay at my house and play after school. His Daddy would pick him up after work on his way home from the mill.

Ronnie and I were almost two years older than the rest of the kids. My parents were missionaries for a year and a half so I got a late start. I was small until I hit puberty so I looked the same age as the other kids. Ronnie got a late start because his folk just forget to send him to school. Ronnie was big for his age and everyone assumed he had flunked a few grades.

Everyone said all the Wilsons looked alike. That was not even close to being true. Mom said there were two sub-species of Wilsons. There were the beefy Wilsons and the scrawny Wilsons. No one saw either species as attractive. The beefy ones were big and muscular, or big and fat. The men had black hair and it covered them from head to toe.

The scrawny Wilsons were either scrawny and tall, or scrawny and short. They often were red headed, and were covered in hair too. The women of the scrawny Wilsons were spectacular redheads and all were short. The beefy Wilson women were all just plain fat. My friend Ronnie was a beefy fat Wilson who turned into a muscular Wilson on his 14th birthday. His Dad was a scrawny tall Wilson and his Mom was an outsider, I think. She died or left before I ever knew Ronnie.

Mom was a native of Marshall City, so was naturally prone to dislike the Wilsons. She somehow liked Ronnie and he liked her. Ronnie's Dad was always polite to her and liked Ronnie to be at our house. When Ronnie was 16, he talked about quitting school and going to work. Mom would have none of that and Mr. Wilson agreed with her. She was an educated woman and might have been seen as an alien from outer space by the Wilsons, but she had a good schoolteacher's manner. She expected obedience and the Wilsons more or less expected to obey.

Ronnie didn't do as well in school as I, but he did pass everything. Most of the town viewed this as a miracle. I helped him with homework and he helped me with social problems. We had some bullies in school and Ronnie had a good way of handling them.

Ronnie and I had our share of boyhood sex play, "you show me yours and I'll show you mine" stuff. When we got to be in our teens, we were touching and I figured out masturbation and gave Ronnie lessons.

He was the only child of his father and he spent so much time with us he didn't get to play with his cousins. I'm sure they figured it out a lot earlier than me. Our timid explorations of sex were my only sexual activity. I was a science geek and really good academically, but not skilled socially.

Everything was fine in my life until the middle of my freshman year in college. When I came home for Christmas break, Mom was feeling feel poorly and had lost some weight. I began to hear people whispering when we went to the grocery store, "I hardly recognized her."

I thought Mom and Dad hadn't noticed, but they did. This was at a time when people didn't mention cancer and they wanted to spare me. It was just after I came home for the summer vacation when they told me they would have to go to Richmond for an operation. At that time, no one thought of talking about female problems with a young male especially when the problem was breast cancer. Boys weren't supposed to know about women's things. Our neighbors, the Browns, would look after me. I didn't like this because I was already 20 and could take care of myself.

Mom and Dad left and Mr. Brown had a stroke the next day and then both of the Browns went off to the hospital. Ronnie was with me so I went home with him, into the depths of Hillbilly Hollow. Before I went with him, I called Dad. He said it was okay. I knew Mom's sickness distracted him, because he never would have agreed normally. I gave him the phone number of one of Ronnie's relatives. He had a phone, unlike Ronnie's Dad.

Ronnie's house had running water and electricity but not much else. It was neat and clean, but bare and sparsely furnished. Mr. Wilson cooked dinner of beans and franks and then went out to the porch to smoke. Ronnie and I cleaned up, talked for a while and went to bed. It wasn't air conditioned so we lay naked on the bed talking and playing with our cocks.

"Are you okay?" Mr. Wilson asked, looking in the door. I almost jumped out of my skin. I was never so embarrassed in my life.

"Sure Dad," Ronnie said, "We're fine." Mr. Wilson looked us over closely and then smiled.

"I can see that," he said. "Don't do anything I wouldn't do." I didn't know what he meant by that, but he laughed, closed the door and left us alone.

Later that night I went to the bathroom and saw Mr. Wilson naked on his bed asleep. I had never seen my father naked, in fact I rarely saw him dressed informally. I couldn't believe grown men would sleep naked. I also didn't believe the size of his cock. He was a scrawny Wilson, but his cock seemed huge.

It was Saturday. I was on summer vacation from school and Ronnie was between classes at the vocational education program at the community college. Mr. Wilson had the day off. He made breakfast. He was a lot better at bacon and eggs than beans and franks. He did some chores and Ronnie and I went exploring. I had never spent any time in the hollow. Caves, tree houses and hideaways filled the place.

Lunch was sandwiches. Two of Mr. Wilson's brothers appeared. Johnny and Joey were big Wilsons and must have been a good ten years older than Mr. Wilson. Joey said his sons, Charlie and Scooter were coming home and would like to get together.

"I've got the boys here," Mr. Wilson said. "I don't want them to be alone. Bobby is the Preacher's son. By the way, Bobby's Dad will call you Johnny if he has to get with Bobby." That was fine with him.

"They're old enough if they want to join in," Johnny said. "You talk to them. It will be more fun if you come." Mr. Wilson's brothers were friendly. Johnny looked a bit like Santa Claus with a big white beard. Joey was a big bear like man with a smile and a funny sense of humor. He had a big black beard. I think I had seen him in town. He was a grease monkey at the Gas Station.

"I'll think about it," Mr. Wilson said. The brothers left. It was getting to be hot and Mr. Wilson said it was time for a siesta. Ronnie's bedroom was on the south side of the house so it was boiling. I figured Ronnie and I could spend the afternoon playing with our cocks. Ronnie had the exact same idea. We usually thought alike.

"Are you boys too hot?" Mr. Wilson asked as he poked his head in the door again. Ronnie and I had just gotten our cocks stroked to a raging hard on when he looked in the room.

"It's okay Dad," Ronnie said as he pulled the sheet up quickly. Mr. Wilson stood at the door, stark naked.

"We're all guys here, Ronnie. My room's cooler and I got a good fan," he said. "Don't be shy; we've all got the same equipment." Reluctantly we followed him to his room. It was cooler.

"I'd like to tell you boys some things, if you can keep them private. Can you do that, Bobby? Ronnie?" he asked. I said sure. Ronnie nodded.

"I take it you guys like to play with each others cocks?" he said. "Well, I have a warm spot for cocks too. As a matter of fact, most of us here do. My Grand Daddy discovered sex with men was as much fun as with women and you didn't have as many strange looking kids that way. You've heard people talking about us in the town, haven't you, Bobby? You know, Cousins Hatcher and Ovid?" I nodded. Hatcher and Ovid were odd-looking men who wandered the streets.

"We get together and enjoy ourselves from time to time and let some steam off. You know the same sort off steam you boys were building up in bed a few minutes ago. That is what Johnny and Joey were talking about tonight. We're having a get together. You are free to come if you want. You don't have to mind you," he explained. "It's for those who like cock play, not watchers."

"What do you do at the party, Mr. Wilson?" I asked.

"Pretty much like the things you and Ronnie were doing," he said. "Call me Frank, not Mr. Wilson. I keep on thinking Grand Daddy is here."

"Is that all you do?" Ronnie asked.

"Nope, I guess you could say we do anything that makes your cock feel good," Frank said. "There are lots of ways to do that and I guess we've figured out most of them by now." I wasn't sure about the whole thing. I couldn't visualize myself in such a group, but the idea excited me. Ronnie was unsure too, but his cock was rock hard. I was just as hard.

"Who's going to be there?" Ronnie asked. His father laughed.

"Some cousins, some uncles, one or two guys from town will be there," he said. "It's a club for the cock hounds. Bobby, in town they call them the sexually active guys. Here they are the guys who can't keep their cocks in their pants."

"How many of your relatives are cock hounds?" I asked.

"As far as I can tell, all of them are, Bobby," Frank said. "It's a sad fact, but all of us are. Grand Daddy figured its better to shoot your load in your Uncle's mouth than a cousin's cunt. It may sound kind of crude, but it works. Cousin Wilburt was caught poking his dick into his sister's business and Uncle Johnny straightened him out." Frank paused in his story.

"I've got to warn you," he continued, "this ain't no ladies club meeting. Wilburt is one horny bastard and he couldn't shoot another load for a week after his first get together. But, he didn't stop smiling either. I wasn't sure you were interested, Ronnie until I saw you boys last night. I figured you were ready now. If you want to come, you're welcome. Johnny and Joey sure were interested."

"What do you mean?" I asked.

"I helped Joey's sons, Charlie and Scooter, learn the ropes. Usually someone takes a new guy under his wing until he learns to fly. Joey helped Wilburt. I helped Joey's boys. Grand Daddy figured no self respecting kid would ever learn anything from his dad. Uncles and cousins work better. Johnny and Joey owe me for helping with their kids. They'd love to help you out."

"You play with Scooter and Charlie?" Ronnie asked.

"I sure do," Frank said. "I guess I've gone too far to not tell you everything. Most of the time it's just fun sex play. Charlie, Scooter and I are kind of close. It's just sex with everyone, except them. We like each other a lot." A horn honked outside. Frank went to the window. It was Johnny.

"Wait a minute and we'll be out!" he cried. We quickly got dressed and went out to the pickup truck.

"I got a call from Bobby's Dad. He needs you to call him," Johnny yelled. I immediately lost my erection, dressed and ran to the car. Frank didn't have a phone, so Johnny had the nearest one. I called Dad. He said the operation had gone well, but he was waiting to talk with the Doctor. He would call as soon as he could.

I asked Johnny if I could wait for the call, he said sure. His house was bigger than Frank's and was filled with stuff. It was hot and Johnny got me a coke. He returned with a coke and without a shirt. His beard was all white, but his chest hair was pepper and salt with a big white patch in the middle. He was muscular and tanned. I think he was a lumberjack.

He was really sympathetic about my mom. He knew a lot about cancer and told me what was happening. His wife had died of the same thing five years earlier. Surprisingly this made me feel better. He also told me what you were supposed to do. No one had said a word about what cancer was. It had just barely occurred to me my Mom could die. It was better to know what was going on.

There was lots of honking outside. It was Scooter and Charlie in a bright red, brand new pick up. They worked in Richmond as carpenters and were doing well. Scooter was a big Wilson. He looked like a younger version of his Daddy. Charlie was a tall, scrawny Wilson with bright red hair and a matching beard. They were shirtless. The phone rang. I ran in and it was Dad.

He said there were many tests to do before they knew exactly how serious it was and they would be in Richmond for at least a week. He asked how I was doing and I said things were great. Everyone was nice and not to worry about me. He said great and he would call me the next day at six in the evening, if that was all right with Johnny. I ran out and asked Johnny. He said sure. It was no problem at all. I told Dad and we said good-bye.

Scooter said he would drive me back to Frank's house. He wanted to show them the new truck. I jumped in and we left.

"Sorry about your Mom. It's real tough," Scooter said. "Daddy told us all about it."

"Thanks. Dad said the operation was good, so I guess things could be worse," I said. "Your Uncle Frank told me you all were having a party tonight." I had no idea where that comment came from. I was thinking about Mom and Dad and this thought came to me. Scooter slowed down and stopped.

"Uncle Frank told you about the get togethers?" Scooter asked. "Are you into that kind of stuff?"

"I really don't know," I said, "I've messed around with Ronnie some. I didn't think I was interested at first, but the idea sort of grows on you."

"I wasn't too sure either the first time," Scooter said. "I thought it would be sort of gang rape. A long time ago, it was with younger boys and was rough. One of the mothers found out and shortened her hubby's cock by three inches. He lived, but learned his lesson. The guys now need to be full growned and willing."

"It turned out to be lots of fun. My brother, Charlie, went first. He told me a lot about what they did, but telling ain't close to doing or feeling. The first time Uncle Frank sucked my cock I couldn't believe anything felt so good. Charlie and I had jerked off together, but I never thought what it was like to shoot a load while someone sucked your cock. Damn, it was good."

"Did you have to do anything?" I asked. "I'm not sure I want to suck a cock."

"I didn't have to do anything, but I did," Scooter said. "It was strange at first. I knew Charlie and I liked to play with our cocks, but I had no idea anyone else did, least of all my Uncles. It was hard to believe Grand Daddy would be moaning in pleasure as Cousin Wilburt fucked him. Frank eventually fucked me too, but that was only after I told him I had an itch up my ass I couldn't reach."

"Were you shocked? Disgusted?"

"I guess I was shocked and turned on," Scooter mused. "Fifteen minutes later the shock was gone, but I was still turned on, big time. I've been turned on ever since. What was hardest to get used was being an adult. This is real man sex, not boy play." He started the car again and we continued on to Ronnie's house.

Chapter 2

Ronnie and I talked over things when I got back. Neither of us was too sure of what we were getting into. For the first time in my life, I let my cock do the thinking for me. Ronnie was curious about who would be there and wanted to see their cocks. I was interested too.

It seemed as if half the guys in the Hollow went around shirtless. I had never seen a grown man bare before I saw Mr. Wilson naked, except for a quick view of Coach Allen in the locker room after a game. I wanted to see and know more.

Mr. Wilson made dinner again. It was hamburgers and he must have been the world's worst cook. Ronnie loved having dinner at my house and now I understood why.

"I think Bobby and I would like to go along with you tonight," Ronnie said. "Is it still okay?"

"It sure is," Frank replied. "I'm glad to have you along." We left about an hour later; driving up the Hollow to a building, they called the Hunt Club. It was a shack with a metal roof and a big porch. It had no electricity and only water from a well. Inside it had a big fireplace on the side and a trestle table in the middle of the room. There were two oil lamps providing dim illumination.

Around the edge of the room were beds covered in animal pelts or quilts. Animal heads covered the walls. The animals were mostly deer, but with several bears and other wild animals mixed in. Johnny, Joey, Scooter and Charlie were already inside. There were three or four other men I didn't know. There was beer and coke. I had a coke. Ronnie had a beer. Two men entered. It was Coach Allen and Dave Anders. Dave had been the captain of the football team a while back and now was a State Trooper.

Most of the guys were beefy Wilsons, except for three men who were Clancies. The Clancies were married into the family and they must have provided the scrawny gene pool. They were ratty looking.

Joey was telling me the story behind one of the animal heads when I saw Scooter taking off his clothes with Frank, Ronnie's father. They put their clothes in a small chest sitting beside a bed and Scooter dropped to his knees and began to suck Frank. No one seemed to pay any attention and we all kept on talking. The light was dim. You could see what was going on more or less, but nothing was spot lighted.

A few minutes later, I saw a Clancie stripping and pairing up with Coach Allen.

"I looks like fun, doesn't it, Bobby?" Joey whispered. He was unbuttoning his shirt. Ronnie came over to us. He already had his shirt off. He was with his Uncle Johnny. I began to take my shirt off. Before I knew it, I was naked and my cock had vanished into Joey's mouth.

I must have been the most nervous person in the world in the time between getting naked and Joey's tongue touching my cock. By the time my cock head was nearing his tonsils, I knew it was going to be a good night. Until then, I thought cock sucking was unnatural, a strange thing no one in his right mind would do.

Joey was a big hairy man with a huge beard, but he had a mouth made for sucking cock. No one had sucked me before, but I instinctively knew this was good. In the back of my mind, I was afraid I was gay. If being gay meant Joey could suck my cock, I didn't care. Joey licked my balls and ass hole; that was another thing I never thought of doing. By the time, his wandering tongue returned to my oozing cock, I was willing to do anything he asked. I knew Joey would be my guide to the world of man sex.

"Do you want to shoot now, or slow up and pop later?" Joey whispered to me.

"What will make it last?" I asked. He looked up from my cock. It was a pink shaft enveloped in his huge black beard. Joey's blue eyes twinkled in the light of the oil lamps.

"We'd better slow up some then," he said, "You're damn near shooting now." He got off the floor and joined me on the bed. I got a good look at him naked for the first time. His cock seemed huge, bloated and oozing.

"Shit, it's big!" I exclaimed without thinking. He looked pleased.

"We Wilsons aren't pretty, but we got the equipment." Joey said. "Grandpa said his Momma got screwed by a donkey and we got the donkey's dick as well as donkey good looks. You can touch it, if you want." My hand was on his cock before I had a chance to say I wasn't going to touch it.

"Play with the balls too," he said, "They're the size of green apples, real baby makers. I hope you don't mind, I'm a real oozer. It makes my cock messy, but tasty." I was spreading his cock ooze over the head with my finger and discovered I didn't mind if it was messy. I stroked his cock and a bead of ooze emerged. This was all new to me.

"Taste it," Joey said. I thought that would be gross, but did it anyway. I had to admit tasting the stuff oozing from a guy's cock didn't appeal to me in theory, but it was good in practice. The ooze was somewhat sweet and a little salty. It turned me on more.

"You liked it, didn't you?" he asked. I nodded. "It's the food of the gods," he added. "Yours is good too." I hadn't realized I was leaking. I wasn't as hard as I had been when he was sucking me and the stuff was dribbling from my piss slit. Joey shifted his place on the bed so he could lick it up. I got hard again.

Ronnie was on the other side of the bed. He was moaning the way he does before he shoots. Normally I like to watch his cum spray all over his body, but Johnny's mouth hid his cock. Johnny's big white mustache rested on Ronnie's thick, black pubic bush. There was no sign of Ronnie's pulsing cock. A minute later Ronnie was asleep and Johnny stopped sucking.

"That was good," Johnny said, "but I'd love to do more. I hope he's not done."

"Don't worry," I said. "Ronnie can cum three or four times. He rests, and then is ready to go in ten or fifteen minutes." Johnny got up and stood next to me with his cock at eye level. He was uncut and half to three-quarters hard and his cock peaked out of the skin with a little cock dribble oozing from the slit. I was sorely tempted.

"Don't be shy," Johnny whispered. "It's made for sucking." I sucked it. Again, the idea was gross, but the actual sucking was great. In fifteen minutes, I had gone from a virgin to a confirmed cocksucker. I was afraid Joey would be annoyed I was sucking his brother when he had done all the work. He wasn't.

After a little while, Joey replaced Johnny and Johnny caught his breath. I wanted to suck more and Ronnie was near enough. His cock tasted different. I guessed it was leftover cock drool from when his Uncle sucked him off. It was good too.

"Give me a little rest, Uncle Johnny," Ronnie mumbled. He opened his eyes and saw me nursing his dick. He smiled. Our eyes met and we both knew our bedroom at his Dad's house would never be the same. He liked what we were doing as much as I did. Soon, I was sucking Joey and Ronnie was at my cock when I shot for the first time that night.

After that, the four of us rested and I went to see what was happening elsewhere in the room. It was quiet. Two men were talking in the middle of the room; everyone else was on a bed to the side. Frank was with Charlie and Scooter. I couldn't tell exactly what they were doing, but I knew three mouths and three cocks were in close proximity somewhere in the tangle of men.

Joey got up and motioned for me to come and meet the men at the table. They were beefy Wilsons. I thought of the local saying that all Wilsons looked alike and realized these guys really looked alike.

"Let me introduce you to the twins," Joey said. "This is Buck and Buster. Boys, this is Bobby. He's Ronnie's friend and this is his first time here." They looked like Bluto in the Popeye cartoons, but seemed friendly.

"Buck has the gold necklace. Buster is the naked one," Joey explained. They were both naked to me.

"Do you work at the recapping shop?" I asked.

"That's us. Covered in dirt and grease most of the time," one of the twins said. "You're in college?" I nodded.

"That's good. We took the jerks' shortcut to fame and fortune," the other twin said. "We dropped out at sixteen. You must be the guy who kept Ronnie in school. Someone in our family needed to finish High School. Ronnie was the one."

"Thank God, what we lack in smarts, we make up in cock," Buck said. "Uncle Joey has been showing you the ropes?" I nodded. I saw Buck fondling Joey's cock. The twins were completely soft. I could see the outline of a cock head halfway up the foreskin. The skin completely hid the head and there seemed to be an inch or two of extra skin. They were hairy, even for Wilson's and the cock skin was the only hairless feature of the tangled mass of black hair at their groins. I could just barely make out the outlines of their balls.

Someone called for Joey, so he left me with the twins. "You guys aren't playing tonight?" I asked.

"We're waiting for Coach Allen," Buck whispered. "We like rasslin, winner fucks the loser. We need a full load to fuck."

"Who wins?" I asked.

"We always do," Buster said. "The coach likes it in the ass, but pretends he doesn't. It's better for him if it's punishment for losing. He really gets off on it."

"Do you ever lose?"

"Not to coach," Buck said, "Frankly, I don't need to lose to like it in the ass. Buster says I have a man-cunt, not a shit-hole. "Feels like velvet," he says." I had never heard anyone talk like that before and I was a bit shocked. Buster felt my cock and my shock turned into an erection. Joey returned.

Joey saw my hard and didn't seem to mind. We talked and Buck slipped to the floor and sucked my dick, then his uncle's, then his brother's. He seemed to like them all. He returned to my cock. He was good. Even though he looked like Bluto, he sucked delicately. A tall, blond man came over.

"Shit, Buck. I didn't think you sucked any cock that wasn't family," he said. "Boy, you must have something special to get Buck to taste foreign food!" he added, looking at me.

"Bobby, let me introduce you to my nephew Wilburt, Johnny's son," Joey said. "He's a loudmouth and a fool, but he has a big cock and is always ready to use it. After all these years of complaining about him, I've gotten to like him." I said hello.

"I like you too, Uncle Joey," Wilburt said with a smile. Buck didn't stop sucking me.

Wilburt was tall and thin. I guessed he was 30 or so. While the hair on his head was thinning, he had a thick mat of curly reddish-blond hair on his chest. A trail of hair connected his chest hair to his pubic bush. His cock was completely soft and hung to his knees. It didn't actually hang that low, but that was the impression. He looked a bit like a scarecrow, but when you took a second look, he was quite muscular. He was missing most of his teeth.

Buck came up for air. Much to my surprise, Wilburt took his place. I was hard by now and Wilburt swallowed me whole. He did something with his tongue and throat that felt good. I thought I was going to shoot a second time, but he pulled off.

He looked up at me sheepishly. "I don't mind cocking the pistol, but I didn't want to pull the trigger this early," he said. "Nice dick you have."

"Your cock is spectacular," I said. Wilburt smiled and rotated so he could suck Buster.

"Wilburt has been a great sucker ever since the truck turned over and he lost his teeth," Buster said. "He's a good fucker too, if you like them big."

Coach Allen wandered over to join our group in the middle of the room. He saw me and blinked. He motioned for me to come over to him. "Bobby, I've never seen you here before," he said.

"This is my first time," I said.

"Enjoying it?" he asked. I nodded and he smiled as he looked at my erection. "I can see that! There's a lot to enjoy here. You can let your hair down and relax." He stroked my cock. "Have you ever seen so many naked men? It's not like the school locker room where everyone is pretending not to look. Everyone here is into it," he said in a whisper. I shook my head. "Nervous?" he asked.

I said yes. "You don't need to be. It's all friendly. No one is going to make you do anything you don't want to. You can watch anyone or anything and try it, if you think you will like it."

"It seems awfully. . . open," I said.

"Let me tell you," Coach said, "I didn't find out what I liked for sex until I was in my thirties. If you have a chance to play with some nice men now, take it. You may never get this opportunity again." He left me and went to Buck and Buster.

"I was wondering if any of you guys would like a nice friendly wrestling match." Coach Allen asked.

"That sounds great to me," Buster said. "We were thinking about a tag team match. You and Buck against Wilburt and me."

"The usual rules?" the Coach asked.

"Sure, but let's add a little fun. What about having the losers taking both of the winners?" Buster said. "Buck said that sounded good to him."

"Then I guess it sounds good to me too," the coach said. Wilburt was getting hard as Allen was staring at the monster meat. It was clear to me the twins were planning for him to screw the Coach.

I wasn't too sure what screwing a man was. Certainly, cock sucking wasn't exactly what I had thought. I wasn't going to complain about cock sucking at all and guessed fucking would be good too. The four men got together, with the two teams working out strategy. The Coach was in charge of the wresting team as well as football, so I assumed he knew what he was doing.

With Wilburt on Buster's team, you just didn't know. Wilburt was one of those people who exuded dumb. He looked as if he didn't have a clue as to what was going on. Johnny stood next to me.

"I still can't believe he's my son," Johnny whispered. "He's a throwback. Looks just like his grandmother's folks."

The match began.

Chapter 3

Wilburt came over to us just before the match started. "Wish me luck, Daddy," He reached down, felt his Daddy's cock and retrieved a finger covered in cock ooze. Wilburt licked it and went back to his partner. Johnny laughed. The match was soon under way and there was a lot of hooting and hollering. It was like a real match, but with all of the wrestlers trying to get their cocks rubbing against the other wrestler.

"He's never lost when paired with the Coach. He hasn't figured it out yet," Johnny said. "He ain't smart, but he turned out to be a nice boy."

"He's really hung," I said.

"Wilburt doesn't have a lot going for him except his cock," Johnny whispered to me. "That's what is good about these get togethers. He's a star here. Everyone loves a big piece of meat and he has it. The first time he came here, he loved it and he's loved it ever since." The wrestlers were all erect now and the match became openly sexual.

Someone rang a bell and the round was over. Buster and Wilburt came over to talk with us. Joey joined us.

"You boys are doing well," Joey said. "It's a lot more like a regular match this time."

"The Coach has never taken Wilburt's meat before. I think he may be having second thoughts," Buster said. Wilburt was fully hard now and he was impressive.

"I'd be surprised if that was a problem," Johnny said. "The Coach is an accommodating kind of man."

"Shit! Everyone here is accommodating," Buster said. "I can't say anyone has said no to anything, ever. Everyone is agreeable."

"It's all in the family," Johnny said, "What's not to like?" In town, everyone said Wilson's Hollow was in another world and it seemed to me they were right. They had been so isolated; they lived by their own rules and didn't know anyone else had any others. Ninety percent of the people in the valley were kin, so it was sex with the family or no sex at all.

As the son of the Presbyterian Minister, to me no sex at all would have seemed to be a reasonable approach. Having no sex wasn't an option anyone in the Hollow seemed to consider. It just didn't occur to them. Sex with men was preferable to women because men couldn't get pregnant. I looked around the room as saw the results of screwing sisters and cousins. There were no brain surgeons in the Hollow. Ronnie, my friend, was smart enough, but I had helped him with enough homework to know book learning was a problem.

It was easy to see the Wilson's as an exotic ethnic group and the party as a strange ritual, like those things you see in National Geographic photographs. No one in the room forced anyone to be there. I was thinking of how much Wilburt liked it. I smiled to myself. The Wilsons were strange, but I liked it too. I didn't have a clue as to what real sex was until that night and what I had sampled already made me a convert.

The events of the night didn't shock me. They seemed interesting, odd, but enjoyable. If Wilson's Hollow was a world filled with easygoing sex, my home was the polar opposite. There was no sex. My parents weren't exactly prudish; it was just they never mentioned sex or even alluded to it. It didn't exist as far as I knew.

I later realized I had few hang ups about sex because I knew so little about it. Dad never discussed it with me. I was a good boy who was never bad. My parents had no fears I would go wild and get a girl pregnant. I don't think they ever would have guessed about Ronnie and me. My only worry as a kid was about being naked. Fortunately, I had been on the track team so I had discovered it was all right to be naked in a bunch of boys in the shower room at least. That little bit of knowledge served me well in Wilson's Hollow.

Several years later in college, I realized the Wilson's sex parties were a combination coming of age rituals and male bonding ceremonies. Once you had participated, you were a man. All men were equal. Older men were elders, or clan chiefs, but they had the same interest in cock as the younger men.

The wrestling match was finishing up. To no one's surprise, Coach lost. Apparently, the fucking was a festive affair and everyone was to gather around. Buck and Buster paired off and in a second, Buster was deep in his brother's ass. I didn't know anything about fucking, but I knew the twins had spent a lot of time fucking before this night.

The main attraction was Wilburt fucking Coach. Wilburt motioned to Ronnie and me to get close. We were new and he wanted us to have a front row seat. That was fine with me. I wanted to see what was going on.

Coach Allen was average height, solid and muscular. He had a crew cut and his brown body hair was even. I later discover this was because he been shaved it and it was growing out. His cock was not as big as many of the Wilsons, but nice. His cock was cut and had a mushroom head. Wilburt told Ronnie and me to hold Coach's legs wide open. Coach wasn't hard, but Wilburt was hard enough for both of them.

Johnny greased up Wilburt's cock and aimed it at Coach's ass. Wilburt poked it in a few inches. Coach winced and his cock turned hard. It was as if a balloon was inflated. Wilburt pulled out and shoved it back in maybe four or five inches. Wilburt had a lot of skin, but on the third or fourth penetration the head was fully exposed.

Coach was oozing a stream of cock juice. He had stopped wincing and had started moaning. Wilburt's dong was still only halfway in the quivering ass. He looked at me, winked and shoved it in to the hilt. Everyone hooted and applauded. I would have thought Coach would have been embarrassed at being fucked in a crowd, but he was moaning in pleasure. I don't think he noticed the audience.

Wilburt was enjoying himself too. "Look at my cock, boys," he said. "Watch my fucker slide into his shit hole. He has a nice, tight ass and he's trying to catch my cock head as it rams him. It's too slippery for him to hold, but it is lots of fun." He pulled out and popped his bloated cock head in the hole a few times. "This feels great," Wilburt explained, "but not as good as this!" He rammed it all the way in. Coach moaned again.

Ronnie and I were hard and dripping as we held Coach's legs and watched the cock relentlessly pound his ass. Wilburt suddenly stopped.

"Would you like to try Coach's ass on for size?" he asked. I was unsure about that. Johnny realized we weren't sure about fucking.

"Go ahead," he said. "Believe me when I tell you, nothing ever bothers Coach as long as he has a cock in his hole." That was enough for Ronnie. Wilburt pulled out and Ronnie slipped in. My friend's cock vanished into the ass and Ronnie began to pump. I looked at Ronnie's face and knew he loved it. He tensed up and shot off after only a few strokes.

"Your turn!" Wilburt said to me. The idea of shoving my cock into the shit hole, as Wilburt called it, wasn't very attractive to me. Everyone was watching and expecting me to do it, so I did. I wasn't greased up like Wilburt and Ronnie, but no one was offering to do it, so I positioned my cock at Coach's ass and pushed. Next thing I knew, my pubic hair was touching his ass. Coach was wide open and his hot rectum enveloped my cock.

I started to shiver it felt so good. I had visualized shoving my cock through shit. Instead, it was a tender, quivering tube. It tightly grasped my cock. The Coach was a hard ass man, but nothing about his ass was hard at all. I have since come to know your ass is defenseless once the cock head breaks past the sphincter. Coach made no effort to stop me.

Guys in the locker room at school talked about being fucked as if it was painful, degrading and humiliating. That was nothing like Coach and me. He was willingly letting my penis into his body. My most private part was touching his most private parts.

That turned me on, but I found a slow pace of thrusting left me near shooting, but not quite getting there. It was great. Most of the audience went back to their own partners, so I was alone with Coach Allen, Wilburt and Dave Anders, the State Trooper.

"You found the grove, Kid," the Trooper said.

"What?" I said like an idiot.

"It's hard to fuck without shooting your load," he explained. "Once in a while, you find exactly the right pace to keep it going for a long time. You've found it. It's beautiful when it happens."

"I hope he doesn't get tired of me," I said. Dave smiled. He was a blonde-haired person and crew cut like the coach, but he was going bald. I think he had more hair in his trimmed, but bushy mustache than on his head. Dave had a cut cock and beautiful balls, dangling from his golden bush. I thought he was smooth when I first saw him, but the whitish-blond body hair was hard to see in the dim light.

"I wouldn't worry about that much. Coach is a big boy. He can take a lot of fucking and still come back for more," the trooper said. "Have you been fucked yet?"

"Nope," I said. His eyes met mine.

"You're not sure about getting fucked, are you?" he asked. I didn't know what to say.

"Don't rush anything, you've got lots of time, no need to rush things," Dave continued. He got close to me and whispered. "If you want your cherry popped by a real nice, gentle guy, think about me. I kind of like being the first. It's a real turn on for me. The guys I've screwed all decided to be bottoms. They know how good it can be."

"Does it hurt?"

"It does some," he continued, "but believe me when I tell you, you won't mind when I'm done. A Trooper friend of mine helps out. He says we should write a book on it, we're so good." I wasn't sure about Dave's offer, but I began to shoot. It wasn't an explosive orgasm. It was slow and lasted a long time. Coach knew I was shooting and squeezed his ass in rhythm with my ejaculations.

I pulled out of Coach's ass and Dave took my place.

"When was the last time you had this much young cum in your ass, Coach?" he asked.

"The tournament in Blacksburg?" Allen asked. Dave laughed.

"Tournaments have always been good," the Trooper said. "Nothing will ever equal the one in Charlottesville. You made a lot of guys happy at that one!"

Wilburt was standing next to me. "Dave's a good guy. You'll like it," he said. "He's done Buster and Buck. They loved it. Shit, they still love it!"

It was getting late and Ronnie and Frank motioned to me they were leaving. Everyone had shot off a few times and the night was coming to a close. Several men were dozing; others were quietly sucking, or slow pumping. I got dressed and said goodbye. We got in the car and drove away.

"How often do you get together Mr. Wilson?" I asked.

"Are you ready to do it again?" he asked.

"You know Daddy," Ronnie said, "I thought that was enough sex for a life time when we left. Now we're a mile away, I'm ready to do it again, tomorrow, or sooner, if possible."

"I guess I feel the same way," I added. We all laughed. When we got home, I was ready to practice some of the new skills I had learned, but fell asleep the minute my head hit the pillow. I woke with the smell of bacon frying. Ronnie woke at the same time. I wanted sex, but was so hungry we both went to the kitchen and ate a good breakfast. Breakfast was definitely Mr. Wilson's specialty.

It was Sunday, so Mr. Wilson took me to church. Everyone there was worried about Mom and Mr. Brown who had the stroke. Mrs. Brown had a heart condition, so the church helped them full time. Dad and Mom were in Richmond and the Browns were in the local hospital and needed as much help as they could get. Everyone was too uptight to talk about breast cancer, so I told them I was doing fine and that satisfied everyone.

The substitute minister was a retired man who preached on sin and the evils of the modern world. My father never liked the man and I realized how bad things were when the church was stuck using him even as a substitute. He was one of those preachers who spouted numbers, such as John 15, verse 12, but never told you what they said. "John 15, verse 12 is further amplified by Matthew 2, verse 18 and then fully explained by Numbers 34, verse 1," he would say. Rev. Billings drove me crazy.

Mr. Wilson and Ronnie picked me up afterward and we went to my house to make sure everything was all right. I found some food in the refrigerator we need to eat, or it would go bad, so we took it to Wilson's Hollow. This included a chicken, ham and a roast. We also stopped at the KFC and got some fried chicken for lunch. I paid for it, with some of the money my parents left for me.

We stopped by Johnny's house and I called my Dad. He was there, back from the hospital and said Mom was doing as well as could be expected. I didn't like the sound of that, but he didn't elaborate. I told him of the church service and the Brown's condition. He laughed at my description of Rev. Billings' sermon. He said Mrs. Brown was prone to fall apart emotionally and they needed to help her.

He told me he had more offers of hospitality than he could accept. He went to seminary in Richmond and knew many people there. He was worried about me, but I said I was fine. It was a good place for me to be. Mr. Wilson and his relatives were as nice as they could be.

We got back to the Wilson's house by 1:30, ate the chicken and had a lazy afternoon. It was hot, so we went to a swimming hole and swam. When I got home, I offered to cook dinner. I had never cooked before, but I had watched Mom and I figured no one could be worse than Frank. I cooked the ham and made baked potatoes. They had fresh beans from the garden. It was simple, but was a hit with Ronnie and his dad.

Frank and Ronnie wore as few clothes as possible in the summer. Washing clothes was a chore. The metal roof on the house made it oven-like in the daytime. The near nudity was hard for me to get used to, since my parents were fully dressed all the time. Wilson women tended to stay inside and wouldn't wear bras. They seemed to stick to themselves, at least in this part of the Hollow.

The men favored cutoff jeans, worn with no shirt and as much pubic hair showing as they could manage. Joey, Johnny and Frank's part of the clan didn't seem to wear briefs and they liked a nice worn area clearly outlining their cocks and balls. Frank went naked until after breakfast and wore boxers around the house. He had the old-fashioned button up type with most of the buttons gone.

I got used to seeing his cock all the time. I was uncomfortable wearing the full Wilson regalia, so I compromised by wearing Bermuda's with no underwear.

We were sitting on the porch one evening a few days later, when a large Cadillac with Tennessee plates drove in. It wasn't new, but it was beautifully maintained and had just been washed. It sparkled.

"Damn! If it isn't Jesse!" Frank exclaimed. He rushed to greet the man. Ronnie told me it was another Uncle. Jesse was the oldest of the brother and had gone to Tennessee and made a lot of money as a welder. Three men got out of the car. Jesse was about 65, five feet ten, 260 pounds, with a white beard. The second man was about 45, five ten, 240 with a pepper and salt bear. The third was 25, five ten, 220, and had a pitch-black beard. There was no question; they were father, son and grandson, a matching set.

"Bobby, this is my brother, Jesse, his son Jesse Junior and his son Jesse III," Frank said, confirming the obvious. They were a bit surprised to see me there. Frank explained my situation and the three men were sympathetic. Uncle Jesse had lost his wife to breast cancer two years earlier.

Ronnie and I went off to get some special brew from a small out building to the rear. They were deep in conversation when we got back. They had all stripped off their shirts by this time and I passed the jug around.

"I can't believe I missed it!" Jesse said. "I made this special trip and missed it. I thought we always had it on Wednesdays."

"We changed it when Scooter and Charlie got jobs in town. They had trouble getting here, so we moved it to Saturday," Frank explained. "I'm sure we can figure something out." As he said that, a State Trooper Patrol cruiser drove up. Jesse's family looked worried. I knew it was Dave and another short man who didn't look like a Trooper at all. He was dressed in jeans and a plaid shirt and had a huge main of curly, blondish-red hair, a handlebar mustache and a red beard.

Frank introduced everyone. Dave's friend was Rod, an undercover agent in Tidewater. Frank knew him, but no one else did. Dave took some of the home brew and complimented Frank on it. I guessed liquor law enforcement wasn't on the agenda for today.

"Rod showed up unexpectedly," Dave said. "I made a little proposition to your son and Bobby on Saturday and I was hoping they were interested. Since you have company, I can try some other time." Frank knew exactly what Dave was talking about. "Rod has to go back tomorrow."

"This may be your lucky day," Frank said. "Jesse and his boys came by for the party and had the wrong day. We just may be able to work something out."

Chapter 4

"Dave has a warm spot for popping cherries," Frank explained to his brother. "He does it so nice; he has a reputation for making it special. Rod's taking lessons."

"This is your lucky day," Junior said. "We just discovered Jesse III shares the family interest. We'd thought he was straight as an arrow and found out different." Jesse III blushed. "He'd been trying out the rest stops. I figured it would be better if he learned it from the family. I had hopes someone from the family would open him up."

"Dave's taken so much Wilson cum over the years, he's almost a member. I think Ronnie's the only one of us who hasn't dropped a load in his ass," Frank said. "That is, until you boys arrived. If you want to try them out, they're willing. They've never said no to a Wilson cock. Dave and Rod are really open-minded for cops."

"Is it my open mind you liked?" Dave asked. "I always thought it was my ass you had a hankering for." Dave and Rod were unbuttoning their shirts. Ronnie later told me, he could smell the sex in the air. Everyone was horny and eager to play.

No one asked if we wanted to be fucked; we all knew. All of us went inside the house and stripped naked. Dave and Ron stood out in the mass of naked men. We were in the middle of a cluster of big and beefy Wilsons. Their dicks were beefy too, thick and meaty. Dave and Ron were slimmer and had long thin cocks. Both men had low hangers, very different from the tight, hairy, ball sacks of the Beefy Wilsons.

I had watched the fucking after the wrestling match. I enjoyed every second I spent in the Coach's quivering ass, but I didn't know what Coach felt. He liked it, but why, I had no idea. I was excited and a bit scared.

There was some confusion. We were short one thin cocked man. It seemed it was against the rules for Frank and Junior to fuck their sons. Rod took Ronnie and Dave took Jesse III. Frank came over to me with Junior.

"I'm a bit big for a first ride, but if you're interested I'm game," Frank said. "Junior would like to help too. But you don't need to, if you don't want to." I glanced down at their swelling cocks. "Feel them if you want." I did. "Hefty, aren't they. Do you think you could take them? I know we ain't family, but we're nice guys."

I didn't want to, but I needed to. I was fully erect now and desperately wanted to know what a cock felt like in my ass. I nodded. In a few minutes, I knew my best friend's father would have his cock in my ass. We went to Frank's bedroom. He told me to lie down.

"Would you like me to grease him up for you?" Junior asked.

"Sure, and take your time about it," Frank said. "Wind him up."

"Has anyone touched your ass hole before?" Junior asked. I shook my head. He touched my hole with a finger. The lubricant was cold and I shivered. He ran his finger around the edge of my hole and then concentrated on the opening. "That's good, you're shivering," he said, "The more excited you are, the better it will be."

He took some of the precum oozing from my cock with his finger and used it to lube me. His finger's activities solely focused on my hole and he was applying pressure. I was relaxing some.

"Daddy loves to be fingered. My cock doesn't fit his ass well, but fingering drives him crazy," Junior said. "Sometimes I shoot a load at his hole and then shove the cream into his ass with my finger. He loves it."

"I thought you didn't mess with your Daddy," I said. He had popped his finger through the ass ring and was lubricating the inside of my ass. It felt good.

"We didn't until after Momma died. Dad was so lonely; I just wanted to help him out. We never played together until I was older," the big man said. "He ate my load after Jesse III was born. He said he wanted to taste the scuz that made his grandson. Damn if I didn't get a hankering to eat his." It seemed to me this thinking was strange, but his finger was getting deeper in my ass and I didn't know if the story or the finger was turning me on.

"Daddy finally said I might as well take it the same way Momma did."

"He fucked you?"

"He sure did," Junior said. "It was good. He's got just about the same meat as my Uncles, except for Uncle Frank, of course. It was real nice."

"You didn't get his cum then?" I asked.

"Well. I actually had already tried it. Wilburt wanted to eat his Daddy's seed, so I sucked Uncle Johnny and he sucked my Daddy. We didn't swallow, so we traded later." Junior said. I was rock hard now and his finger was in deep.

"You boys!" Frank said. "I remember that night. I thought you were up to something!" He seemed amused. "Junior, why don't you try stretching his hole with your cock head? Yours is smaller than mine, he might like it better."

"Are you ready?" Junior asked. I nodded. He raised my legs and positioned his cock at my ass. The head nuzzled in my hole. He was applying some pressure, but not a lot. "Frankly, the idea of letting a guy shove his cock in my ass didn't have much appeal to me at first. The idea grew on me." Junior continued. "I'm not going to fuck you, Bobby. I just have my cock at your hole. If you relax, it will slip in. Just think of it as opening the door for a friend."

"Everyone likes to fuck, but the feelings can be really good when you get fucked. I didn't believe it at first, but it's true," he said. I was wiggling my ass to get more comfortable. I found a good position and I realized his head was completely in my ass.

"Damn it Frank! I'm in already!" Junior said. "I didn't mean to go all the way. I hope you don't mind."

"Don't wait for me," Frank said. "Fill him up and I'll do a refill later."

"Do you mind?" Junior asked me. I told him to go ahead. It didn't hurt, my ass just felt full. Junior slipped in deep slowly, giving me a chance to get used to it. He began to pump slowly. I was thinking it felt okay, until it began to feel a lot more than okay. Junior began to moan.

"Shit, Junior," Frank exclaimed. "I can't believe you still have a hair trigger!" Junior twitched a good long while and then pulled out.

"Are you done for the night, or do you feel like some more play time?" Frank asked me. He stroked my cock and knew the answer. I was rock hard.

"I'm not sure," I said. "It was just beginning to feel good."

Frank smiled. I could hear Ronnie moaning in the other room. Rod must have been in Ronnie's ass by then and Ronnie was enjoying it. Frank didn't say anything, he just lubricated his cock and got my legs on his shoulders the way Junior had.

He was in all the way in a split second. I couldn't breathe. He pulled out and shoved in again. After two or three more repetitions, my cock twitched and shot out a squirt of cum. Frank stopped.

"Try and relax and stop it!" he ordered. I tried to do as he asked and stopped my orgasm. I couldn't believe I could do that. "Just relax. Calm down," he said, "If you don't pop now, I can fuck you for a long time. It will feel great." It did feel good. It was different from anything I had felt before, as if someone was jerking me off from inside my body.

"Junior, you did a wonderful job opening him up. It's smooth a silk inside," Frank said.

"It's my sperm!" Junior said. "It's always good when you use cum to grease the chute. I shot a big load. I'd saved it for almost a week."

"Whatever it is, it sure does the trick," Frank replied. He looked at me. "You're even better than Charlie and Scooter." He was smiling. "It took them some time to get used to my donkey dong. You like it on the first time. You're going to be a great bottom." Frank said that as a compliment. He started thrusting again.

Frank was right. It did feel good. His cock was huge and it squeezed everything that liked to be squeezed in my ass. It got better as he continued to pump my hole.

I started to wiggle to force his cock into unexplored areas. Frank liked that. He adjusted his thrusts to match my undulations. I had not thought of him as a smart man, but he knew my ass perfectly. I was going crazy. I wanted to shoot, but couldn't do it. It felt so good it almost hurt.

Frank slowed up for a minute and asked me if I wanted to try it doggy style. I said sure, so we tried that for a while. It was good too, but it was better on my back. On my back, he could stroke my cock. Ronnie and Rod came in to watch. Frank suddenly pulled out and shot his load on my cock. It was a big one, coating my dick and balls with his jiz. It was exciting, but I missed having a cock in my ass.

Rod must have been a mind reader. He slipped in as soon as Frank was done. Rod had a long thin cock and it was no problem at all for me. Frank's dong completely filled my ass, so there was no room to maneuver. There was some room to spare for Rod's snake and he probed different parts of my ass.

Frank left for the other room with Junior to see how Jesse III was doing. Ronnie was on the bed beside me. He stared at the sperm dripping from my cock. He leaned over and began to lick it off.

"That's it Ronnie!" Rod said. "Lick your Daddy's cum off your best friend's dick. Clean it up real good." Ronnie straddled me, so we could sixty-nine. He was leaking buckets of pre cum. Rod picked up his pace and began to moan. I began to climax, my cum spurted all over Ronnie's face before he had a chance to stop licking up his Daddy's cum and suck my cock head. He didn't mind. He began to spurt. I think Rod was doing the same in my ass.

We finally pulled apart and rested. I was wiped out, drained. I figured this was enough sex to last me a lifetime. The three of us were on the bed asleep. Dave came into the room. I opened my eyes and he saw me and motioned for me to come over to him. I slipped out of bed without waking Rod or Ronnie.

"How was it?" he whispered.

"It was great," I said. "I loved it."

"Do you have a hankering for another cock?" he asked. "I'd love to take you for a ride." He fondled my cock and balls. I thought I was too tired, but that wasn't true. The minute he touched by balls, I was ready to go again. He led me to Frank's bedroom. In the living room, Junior took Frank's cock while he fingered Jesse's ass. Jesse III was sleeping on the couch.

Dave didn't fuck me; he made love to me. To the Wilson's sex was play, pure recreation. I discovered Dave was taken by me. He was smitten. Dave was handsome, macho and hard as nails on the outside. I was use to sex with the odd-looking Wilsons. I couldn't believe this beautiful man liked me. We kissed, we sucked, we caressed. I was ready for him to fuck me when he straddled me and sat on my cock.

Eventually I guess there was no combination of cock, mouth and ass hole we didn't try out. It was beautiful. I learned the difference between fucking and loving that night. It was wonderful to be with someone who loved you and wanted you. The Wilsons were fine. They liked you and the sex was great, but it was not the same. Dave was a nice man, kind, gentle and caring. He was romantic and loving.

After we had both climaxed, I told Dave what I felt. He said he felt the same.

"The Wilsons are the strangest people I have ever met," he said. "I had a long talk with Johnny once. I had been looking for Mr. Right and would settle for nothing less. I got lost serving a warrant and came upon Johnny and his brothers playing. I was a straight arrow and was going to arrest them, but ended up joining the group."

"Quite frankly, I didn't know you could feel that good. I had been eating peanut butter sandwiches and suddenly I discovered fillet mignon." Dave continued."As a good Baptist boy, I felt guilty as shit afterward. Johnny took me aside and straightened me out. He figured there were three kinds of sex. Baby making sex was dangerous and could get you into a lot of trouble as far as he was concerned."

"Believe it or not, they do understand the problems of intermarriage and having too many mouths to feed. Ronnie, Charlie and Scooter are the first fruits of the family trying to get reproduction under control."

"Ronnie's nice," I said, "and normal."

"Charlie and Scooter are the first guys to have real jobs. Jesse's trip to Tennessee also was a success. They realized they could do well," Dave said. "Johnny also recognized they are as horny a bunch of men as you will find. Messing around solved that problem. They figure, if it doesn't make babies it ain't sex, it's just play."

"It seems like sex to me," I said. Dave laughed.

"It seems that way to me too," he said. "They think of it as a way to let off steam and have fun. It's all in the family because they just don't associate with anyone who isn't family. "Who else are you going to play with?" Johnny asked. They've been isolated here for generations. What they do isn't sex, it fun."

"Sort of like a hunting trip with your brothers, or a trip to Disney World," I said.

"You got it," Dave said. "It's a rite of initiation and bonding experience. It makes the family stronger, in addition to keeping the girls, virgins." Dave paused. "Johnny told me sometimes it was more than just messing around. Sometimes you want to be with a guy you really like. He doesn't think there is anything wrong with loving another man. I don't think there is anything wrong with that either."

"How do you deal with being a Policeman?"

"It's a problem," Dave answered. "I love being a cop and I love men too. I'm screwed, if it ever gets out." Frank opened the door and joined us.

Chapter 5

"Are you boys getting along well?" Frank asked.

"We hit it off just fine," Dave said. "I saw you've been having a good time too. How was Junior?" Frank got on the bed with us. He snuggled up to me.

"Junior and I have always gotten along well. Bobby here is a real find," Frank said. "He's born to bottom."

"Is that good?" I asked. They both laughed.

"It is if you are the bottom and your friends are tops!" Dave said. "You seem to have taken to it like a duck to water." We talked for a while and then fell asleep. I got up just before dawn and went to the bathroom.

Ronnie was in line after I finished. He must have gotten up at the same time.

"How are you doing?" he asked.

"Real good, and you?"

"Fine, Rod was great," Ronnie said. He paused. "How was Dad?"

"He was nice. Junior screwed me first, so I was already open a bit."

"Was it strange?"

"Sort of," I said, "Once it was in, it felt so good, it didn't make any difference."

"That's the way Jesse was. He has nice and thick equipment. It felt good." Ronnie said. "I didn't believe it felt as good as it did. Dave was nice, but Jesse was great. He came over to me after Dave left. He asked if I'd mind. I said it was fine, just to be polite. He sent me to the moon."

"That's the way your Dad was. I've never felt anything like it. It felt like he was jerking me off from the inside," I said. "It got better once I relaxed." Ronnie laughed.

"Those are almost the exact same words Jesse used.""Relax and let me do the driving," he said. It was odd to have someone else in control," Ronnie said. "There was nothing I could do."

"Except feel the pleasure?" I interjected.

"That's it. Damn it was good," Ronnie added. Jesse III must have heard us talking and joined us in the hall in front of the bathroom. "You guys okay?" he asked.

"We're fine, are you?" Ronnie asked.

"Shit, I didn't know things could be that good. I've been messing around the truck stops for a year now and didn't know the mother load of man sex was in my back yard," Jesse III said as he put his arm around me and fondled my cock. "You're the smallest guy here and you took all the big meat. How are you doing?"

"I'm afraid I liked it as much as you did," I said. Jesse III patted my ass and slipped his finger in my hole.

"You took Dad and Uncle Frank, didn't you?" he asked. I nodded. "Dad said you were real nice." We had spent most of the night playing, but I was surprised I was still excited. Clearly, Jesse III was interested. He was already semi erect. I glanced at Ronnie and saw he was in the same state. Dave and Rod came to the bathroom.

They had to get to work, so we broke up and soon were making breakfast for the Troopers. Everyone was up by then, so we all had breakfast. Dave gave me a ride to Johnny's house, so I could call my folks. Dad said they would be home the next day. Mom was doing well, but it would be a long recovery. Looking back, I should have noticed there was something not quite right in Dad's voice. He was practicing the official line he and Mom would have when they returned.

Joey arrived and the two brothers gave me a ride back to Frank's house. They wanted to see Jesse. Jesse and his brood had been planning to return to Kentucky, but after an hour of conversation, they decided to spend another night. Frank was at work until five, but it seemed most of the men in the Hollow had a casual schedule and could take the day off. I said, I would be going home the next day and I needed to go to my house and straighten it up.

I figured it would be nice for Mom to come home to a clean house. Jesse III and Ronnie offered to help, so we all drove home in Junior's big car. I dusted, vacuumed and made the beds. Mom hadn't been doing much housework before she left for the hospital. Ronnie mowed the lawn and Jesse trimmed and pruned the bushes in the yard. They had gotten very shaggy.

I went to make lunch. When I opened the refrigerator, it was a total disaster. It smelled as if something had died. I took out a bottle of something that had gone bad. It slipped from my hand and splattered all over the floor. It was some homemade chicken broth. The stench was unbelievable. It took a good two hours to clean it up and then air out the house.

Ronnie and Jesse III were good sports and by three, the house looked great and even smelled good. We sat down in the living room and rested. It was strange to see the two big men in the formal living room of my house. The phone rang. It was Johnny.

"Are you boys coming home?" he asked.

"Sure. We're finished here," I said. "We'll be there shortly."

"You had a good time while you were here?" Johnny asked. "Junior said you had a good time last night?" Johnny asked. I said, of course I did.

"We were thinking about having another party tonight, like last week end. Are you game?" Johnny asked.

"You couldn't keep me away," I replied.

"My brothers and I were thinking about having a party the way we used to when we were your age. They were a bit more rough and tumble than the parties now a days," he explained. He paused. "The party we had last weekend was tame compared to the old days. Less sucking, more fucking. Do you think you'd be interested?"

"I know I'm interested."

"We've never had anyone who isn't family at one of these parties, but Junior and Frank want you to be there bad," Johnny said, chuckling. "I don't know what you did, but they liked it a lot. You tell Jesse III and Ronnie what we're planning and see if they are interested." I put Ronnie on the phone. Johnny explained the plans and Ronnie said, sure. Ronnie turned the phone over to Jesse III. Jesse hung up after a few minutes. He was smiling.

"We're going to have a good time tonight!" Jesse said.

"It sounds good to me!" I said. "Do either of you guys know what it's like?"

"I have some idea," Jesse III said. "Driving over here in the car Dad and Gramps told me about the parties. Did Uncle Frank tell you, Ronnie?"

"Well, he told me some, but I kind of have the feeling he didn't tell me all," Ronnie said. "Why don't you tell us? I'd love to know the whole story."

"Great Grandpa started it," Jesse explained. They said it was because there were too many crazy Wilsons. The Wilsons were always a horny bunch and eventually everyone in the Hollow was kin of some sort. The curse was Wilson women. They get pregnant at the drop of a hat."

"They got pregnant easy, but bearing the baby was another thing. Most girls were knocked up by 14 or 15, but they either lost the baby, died in childbirth, or gave birth to a strange kid. Great Grandpa's favorite sister, Ellie, died at 15 in childbirth. Her baby was deformed and died a month later. Ellie told him it was his older brother who was the father."

"As he got older, he figured the girls got pregnant too early and were knocked up by the wrong man. He was a big man, opinionated and strong as an ox. By the time he was 30, Great Grandpa was the head of the clan. He decided to change things. Daddy said, Great Grandpa liked man sex a lot and had played with his brothers. He decided man sex could solve the crazy Wilson problem and keep the Wilson women alive.

"He found a Preacher man who helped him with the problem. Rev. Oswald Clancy was a fire and brimstone preacher who wandered into the Hollow and set up shop. He preached that sex was evil and bad except to make babies. Originally he preached that all sex was bad, but Grandpa fucked him royally and Oswald loved it."

"Oswald was a smart man. Sex, he said, was for procreation, and was sinful when done for other reasons. Man play wasn't sex, because it couldn't result in a baby, and thus man play wasn't sinful." I laughed.

"Smart is hardly the word for it."

"He was clever and horny as shit," Jesse III continued. Great Grandpa and he were sexual athletes. They liked sex and soon converted most of the men to their way of thinking. They both loved it in the ass and most of the guys discovered it was a hell of lot easier to deposit their seed in a willing man's hole, then to screw a girl and have to deal with after affects.

"Especially if her parents and your own parents were the same!" Ronnie added.

"One hundred percent right!" Jesse III replied. "Rev. Clancy had noted the preference for screwing sisters and daughters. He figured that sons and brothers were a better choice. Keep all the seed in the family was his thought. Daddy said most of the sex was fucking in the old days. Indoor plumbing and bathtubs were rare and the dicks were too ripe to suck most of the time. Several of the clan discovered showering in the Navy, when they were drafted in World War II."

"That must have been a blessing," Ronnie said.

"Daddy said they liked it once they got the hang of it. They had no education and didn't take complicated orders well, but in the Navy, you don't need much to be a stoker in a boiler."

"That must have been awful," I said. "I can't imagine shoveling coal for hours in the boiler room of a ship."

"It turned out fine. They learned to suck cock with the boiler room crew of a cruiser! They've always had a liking for the sea," Jesse III said. "It was fortunate that Great Gramps and Rev. Clancy liked to both pitch and catch. Wilsons could all take as well as give; everyone seemed to share the versatility. Let's just say Wilsons did a lot for the morale on their ships!"

"So what's up tonight? Is it so different from the usual?" I asked.

"Uncle Jesse was telling me, all Wilsons like man sex, but some like it a lot. Tonight it's going to be just the guys who like it a lot. He called it no 'pussyfooting' sex. No rules, just man ramming fun," Ronnie said.

"I didn't know there were that many rules?" I said. "I sure didn't notice any." Ronnie and Jesse III laughed.

"Well we'll all find out," Jesse III said. "It's usually only members of the family, only the real horny ones." There was a brief silence.

"How did Dad's cock feel when he fucked you?" Ronnie asked. I knew exactly what he was thinking about. He hoped his Dad would fuck him.

"I'm new to being fucked, but I'm pretty sure it was about as good as it gets. Junior was good too," I said. I wasn't sure if talking about how your best friend's father's cock felt in your ass was the right thing to do. Ronnie wasn't offended or bothered. He was just curious.

"Your Dad is real big, but nice and gentle. He worked it in slow and easy. At least until he hit a real good spot," I said. "He must have felt me react when he hit it. I think it must have been his cock head rubbing my prostate. Once he found it, he sped up. After he got going, it was so good you didn't know what he was doing. Or care, for that matter."

"Did it take a lot of lube?" Ronnie asked.

"It took a lot for Dave to get in me easily," Jesse III added.

"Not that much, but Junior had already shot his load in me. Junior told me he hadn't shot off in a week and he dropped a big load. You Wilson's have bull balls," I commented. Jesse III smiled.

"A trucker at a rest stop told me, I shoot a full seven course meal, not just the desert, like most guys," Jesse III said. "He wanted me to shoot a load on a sandwich. He thought it would be better than mayo!"

"Did you do it?" I asked.

"Nope. I had just cum and it takes a while to build up again. He said that we could try the next time we hooked up," Jesse III said. "Rest stop sex is kind of hit and miss. So far we have missed."

"You like the rest stops?" I asked.

"When it's the only place you can have sex, I do," Jesse said. "I like truckers. It's fun, fast and easy. Last night was different from anything I have done. It was odd to be having sex and not be afraid of someone catching you. I've never done it with family before. Dad's never done it with anyone but family. It takes some getting use to."

"Well it's time to be going home," I said. "Let's lock up and get a move on it." The house did look good and I hoped my parents would like it. We drove back to Ronnie's house. It was empty. Johnny had left a note saying, "Gone fishing." I took a shower and when I got to the bedroom, Jesse III and Ronnie were sound asleep. I know a good thing when I find it, so I joined them.

The smell of dinner woke me up. The fishing trip was a success and Jesse and Joey were frying the fish. They were good cooks and when Frank got home from work, we all sat down to a good dinner. Ronnie and I washed the dishes after. We heard a knock at the door and there was an outbreak of greetings in the other room.

Johnny brought a tall, thin man to meet us. He was called Slim and he was a reddish blond Wilson. He had a short, very hairy guy with him named Clydesdale. Clydesdale had neatly trimmed hair and a short beard. His plaid shirt was open to his navel revealing a tangled mass of hair, so thick you could hardly see the skin.

"I know this is supposed to be family only," Slim was explaining, "but this party had such short notice. Clydesdale was spending the night and he shares the family interests. I will swear he has Wilson blood in his veins."

"It can get a bit rough and tumble," Johnny said to Clydesdale.

"I ain't no shrinking violet myself," the small man said. "As long as there are some cocks and ass holes available, I'll be just fine."

"You're kind of small," Joey said. "You might get hurt." Clydesdale and Slim laughed.

"Believe me, Clydesdale ain't small where it counts," Slim said.

Joey motioned to me to get closer to him. "Did Johnny tell you usually the men like to try on the new men for size?" he whispered.

"No," I said.

"Junior and Frank said you liked it a lot last night," he continued. "The good part is there is lots of sex. The bad part is there is lots of sex. If you have the right attitude, it will be great."

"Does everyone get to fuck me?" I asked. I was a bit worried.

"That's not the way it works. No ass is off limits. If you see an unfilled hole, you go in. Age and relationships mean nothing," he said. "There will be ten to twelve men here; I wouldn't be surprised if you end up screwed by most." I was uneasy about this, but realized I was already hard. Joey took my hand and placed it on his basket. He was hard too.

"Were you thinking about being first in line?" I said. I was smiling.

"Actually Johnny and I both wanted to take you for a ride," he said. Joey was unbuttoning his shirt. "Why don't we get naked?"

"We're the only ones," I replied.

"I'll promise you by the time my cock touches your hole, everyone will be naked," Joey said. "They're just waiting for the starting gun."

He was right about that. I unbuttoned my shirt as Joey removed his shirt and undid his belt. Johnny must have been watching. His shirt was off before mine. He joined us. The party was underway.

Chapter 6

I was with Joey and Johnny. Joey got on a bed with his head on the edge. He was at my cock height and licked my cock head. I bent over and sucked him. His fat cock was soft when I started, but was oozing precum after three licks. He was ready. This 69 position opened my ass wide and Johnny worked some lubricant into my hole.

His cock was right behind his fingers. The two brothers had similar cocks, uncut, thick and meaty. I had never been sucked while someone fucked me and it was hard to get my feelings straight. There were so many sensations. Joey's cock was in my mouth, rock hard and oozing. With his mouth sucking my cock and Johnny's cock pumping into my ass I was spinning. Joey pushed my legs wider apart, so my ass would be more open.

"Damn! It's a pretty view from here," Joey exclaimed when he was talking a break from sucking me. "I haven't seen you this hard in years, Johnny."

"You could lick my balls if you want a real show," Johnny said. Joey shifted under me, so he could suck his brother's balls. I was still deep throating him. Johnny moaned as Joey licked his balls. Joey began to twitch and suddenly I had a mouthful of Wilson cum to deal with. Joey shot a massive load. Johnny held me tight, never letting his cock leave my ass. I was being front and rear loaded at the same time. Eventually, we let Joey get out from under me. Ronnie had entered the room while I was being fucked. Ronnie got on the bed and replaced Joey.

Ronnie and I were used to 69ing and it was nice to have him there. His cock wasn't as thick, but was a bit longer than his uncles. It was easier to breathe while sucking Ronnie. He was hard, but not oozing.

"Who are yah fucking?" a voice asked. I didn't recognize the voice.

"The preacher's son, Bobby. He's a nice kid," Johnny answered. "When did you get here, Eddie? I hadn't seen you."

"Just a few minutes ago," Eddie answered. "Billy is with me. Wilburt told me it would be okay. Can I spell you a while?"

"Sure," Johnny said. Johnny pulled out and Eddie replaced him. I would have been real uneasy about having a guy I had never met, or seen fuck me, but it was done so fast I didn't have a chance to think about it. Eddie's cock went a lot deeper, but it must have been thinner. It didn't hurt at all.

A hand opened Ronnie's legs and began to lubricate his ass. A few seconds later reddish blond pubic hair appeared, right above another long thin cock. The cock vanished into Ronnie's ass. Ronnie liked it, if a generous spurt of precum is any indication. You can't hide anything from a guy who is sucking you.

I didn't know if it was Eddie or Billy in my ass, but whoever it was, he knew his stuff. It felt good, but not as good as to make me shoot right way. After the thick Wilson cocks' the thinner meat had room to explore my ass. The dick hit different places on each thrust. I think the guy fucking Ronnie was doing the same. Ronnie was oozing good, but some thrusts rewarded me with more precum.

"Shit!" Ronnie's partner exclaimed.

"What's wrong Eddie?" the guy fucking me asked.

"I'm ready to pop already," Eddie said.

"If I've told you once, I've told you a thousand times, you either pull out and cool down, or go for it," Billy said with mock irritation.

"But it feels so good!" Eddie replied. He pulled out. Another cock appeared. This was much bigger, both fatter and longer. It was uncut and dripping. Ronnie's ass was wide open after Eddie vacated it and the new meat immediately filled the void. Ronnie oozed a big glob of precum and moaned. Billy continued to pump his cock into my ass.

"How are you doing, Frank?" Billy asked.

"Just fine. Couldn't be better, Frank said. Ronnie twitched and oozed a bucket full of pre cum as he realized, it was his father's cock deep in his ass. "You got yourself a hot one there." Frank told Billy. "I opened him up for the first time yesterday and he loved it. It's nice to get a virgin that doesn't need any training. Bobby's a natural."

I was sucking Ronnie, but Ronnie had stopped sucking me. My cock was still in his mouth, but nothing was happening. A huge spurt of cum filled my mouth. It had force, like drinking from a hose. Ronnie shot off and tried to eat my cock whole, I popped too. Ronnie and I slurped up each other's cum and we shared our orgasms. Billy was frantically thrusting in my ass and I knew he was shooting too.

We all pulled apart as we cooled down, except for Frank and Ronnie. Frank was still deep in his son's ass.

"Do you want me to shoot in there?" Frank asked.

"I sure do, Daddy!" Ronnie said. Frank was ready; he must have popped a few seconds later.

"That was nice Daddy," Ronnie said. "Real nice."

"It was, wasn't it," replied Frank. "I was afraid I was too big for you to like it. Afraid it might hurt."

"Bobby told me it was good," Ronnie said.

"I'm tired," I said, "how long does the party last?" Frank chuckled.

"It's just begun," Frank explained. "My Daddy never thought a party like this was a success unless he screwed, or had been screwed by every guy here. My Daddy told me to think of my first party as a "Whitman's Sampler" of cock." I must have looked overwhelmed. "You never know which cock will really hit the spot. I went to the moon the first time I played with Scooter and Charlie. I wasn't much of a virgin then and it still took me by surprise."

"What did it feel like?" Ronnie asked.

"You know what it feels like when the cock head rubs your nut?" he asked.

"The prostate?"

"Yah, that's it." Frank answered. "Well, it was like that, but it was my entire shit chute that felt that way. Scooter was fucking me while I topped Charlie. My cock almost exploded. And the nice thing was, they felt the same thing. Granddaddy liked my ass a lot, but he didn't do shit for me. I was polite and everything, but it wasn't a thrill. Charlie and Scooter felt exactly the same way I did."

"Damn!" I said; it did sound good.

"You know, there was no combination of cock and ass hole we didn't try. Everything worked. I must have been in each of their asses a good ten times, and they in mine the same," Frank said. He had a faraway look in his eyes. "Damn, it was good." Jesse came in the room with the small guy they called Clydesdale.

"Ronnie, Junior was looking for you. He and Jesse III want you in a little family confab." Ronnie left, but Clydesdale remained. He was short, very homely, very hairy and horse hung.

"You need to enter that in the county fair," Frank said. "It's a beauty."

"You got some nice equipment yourself," Clydesdale said. He had a deep bass voice. "Interested in giving my cock a spin? Give it a test drive?"

"I sure am, but just shot off a minute ago. I need some time to refuel." Frank responded. "Bobby here is game." Clydesdale looked at me closely.

"I'm not much into young guys," Clydesdale said. He was playing with his cock, stroking it so the cock head would peak from the foreskin. The cock was the only part of his body other than his eyes and teeth that wasn't covered in brownish gray hair. "It takes some experience to appreciate my cock. It's not for beginners."

"Bobby had no trouble with mine," Frank said. "I'm no expert, but I suspect he has all the makings of a bottom who may well be a size queen." Clydesdale looked at me again.

"Do I have anything to say about this?" I asked. Clydesdale smiled. He stroked my cock. It was a lot harder than I thought it was.

"I never go where I'm not wanted," he said, still smiling. "But, it's hard to believe I haven't tickled your fancy. I need a guy real relaxed to take it. If you're tense, it'll never get in." I had to admit, he had more than tickled my fancy. My irritation had turned to curiosity.

"You don't like young guys?" I asked.

"It's not that. My cock ain't made for amateurs," Clydesdale explained. "I don't have time for guys who think they might like to get fucked. I say, lie back, open your legs and go for it. I like to fuck and I like guys who like to be fucked. What more is there?" He continued to stroke my cock. I was oozing a lot of precum by then. He knew what that meant. He raised my legs and nuzzled his cock head in my hole. I shivered in excitement.

Clydesdale looked like your basic, redneck, cock hound, but he was a considerate fucker. He was careful and slow as he worked his donkey dong into my ass. He stopped a few times when it hurt and added lube. It did hurt some, but it got more exciting as he pushed it deeper. When it was fully lodged, Clydesdale stopped for a minute, and then began to pump. After the third or forth thrust, I got really excited, moaning and shivering in ecstasy.

"I told you he was a good boy!" Frank said.

Eventually Ronnie, Jesse III, Slim and I were on the bed. Each of us had our legs raised and spread. Frank, Junior, Johnny, Joey, Eddie, Billy and Clydesdale were taking turns fucking us. Buck and Buster had joined the group at some time as had Wilburt. The three of them seemed to like the bottom too, so they relieved us when it got too much.

Much to my surprise, I was more than willing to get back in the swing of things after a short rest period. The Wilsons may have been sex maniacs, but I sure was able to keep up with them.

It might sound as if this was a wild and crude gang-bang, but it was not like that at all. Johnny had said this party was for the guys who really like sex and he was right. Everyone loved man sex and wanted to see how much fun we could have. It was almost a contest to see who could have the most pleasurable experience. The tops were as interested in the bottoms' orgasms as they were in their own.

During one of my rest periods, I was sitting on a sofa in the living room. Jesse came over and talked to me. He was an old man, but his cock was still thick and he maintained a good erection. I yawned.

"You know," he said, "after the second or third orgasm, the party picks up and gets interesting."

"What do you mean?' I asked. "I'd think you'd get so tired the party would peter out."

"Even men with hair triggers, relax and enjoy themselves after they've popped a few times. Once the initial excitement is gone, you get more cock time," he explained. "You don't need to shoot anymore, so you can enjoy the cock, or the ass. You can take your time and savor the screwing. Plus, it takes more work to make a guy pop the third or forth time. The boys need to be more imaginative."

"It all seems pretty imaginative to me. I never thought I'd be on a bed being fucked by you all," I said. Buster had been listening and joined us.

"We may look like hillbillies, but we've had a lot of time to figure out fucking," Buster said. "I'm not blowing my own horn, but we know screwing forwards and backwards." As if to demonstrate his point, Buster motioned for me to lie back on the couch, so he could have his turn. Buck had screwed me earlier that night, so I figured it would be the same. Buster and Buck were almost identical.

I could not have been more wrong. Buck had a short, thick cock that felt like Johnny's or Joey's. Buster had a huge cock head on a comparatively thin shaft. They were both uncut, so they looked the same soft. Buster's head hurt a little when it popped through my sphincter, but once it was in the shaft could hardly be felt at all.

I could only feel the huge mushroom as it traveled within my ass. It rammed my prostate until it pushed past it, then rubbed it again as he pulled out. I couldn't believe how good it felt. I glanced up at Buster, his eyes weren't focused and he was drooling. He felt the same way.

"Shit," he said, "my cock just fell in love!" I felt that same way. My prostate loved his cock head. Jesse was playing with my tits and Junior had joined us and was playing with my cock.

"Buster, you really have Bobby going!" Jesse said. "I think he's going to pop."

"Do you want his cum?" Junior asked.

"You take it, I've had my share tonight," Jesse said.

"Thanks, Daddy," Junior said, as he swallowed my cock. Buster started to moan as he shot his load deep in my ass. Junior sucked me until I shot. Buster pulled out after he came, but Junior stayed on my cock as I ejaculated.

"Is it good, son?" Jesse asked.

"It sure is," Junior said. "It's good to the last drop." Jesse let go of my tits and moved into the position Buster had just vacated. He lifted my legs and a second later, his cock was in my sperm filled chute. Jesse sighed in pleasure.

"It's smooth as silk in there," he said. "Buster, did you shoot a big load in Bobby?"

"I'm pretty sure I did," Buster said. "I couldn't help it, Uncle Jesse. It just felt so good." Buster was sitting next to me, caressing my hair as Jesse fucked me. Jesse III came into the room. He saw his Grandpa fucking me and Dad sucking my cock. A second later, Jesse III jointed his father and they took turns licking my dick.

Chapter 7

I thought all would be the same when Mom and Dad returned, but they were different. They seemed detached and preoccupied. Mom was weak and the ladies of the church came by regularly to help her out. Everyone said, all was well with the operation, but I knew it wasn't. They tried very hard to be the way they had been before, but that just wasn't possible. In the fall, I went back to college and life seemed more normal.

My sophomore year was good. I was a good student and things went my way. I came home every few weeks. I talked about taking a semester off but Mom would have none of that. I think she had hope she would make it long enough to see me graduate. Mom was getting thinner and weaker. Ronnie came by regularly. He liked yard work and I liked vacuuming, so cleaned on my visits. The house and the yard looked the same as before. Mom was pleased.

Dad got more and more preoccupied. He was really worried and concerned, but didn't seem to be able to cope. He decided to leave the church and find a position in Richmond so they could be nearer the hospital.

He stayed until the church found a new minister and I was packing and studying for final exams.

They were in Richmond looking for a rental house while I was taking my final test in English at the end of the year. Mr. Smithers, the Dean of Students, came to the classroom. He called me out and took me to the office. There was a State Trooper waiting. He said, an eighteen-wheeler had jumped the median of 460 and had hit Mom and Dad head-on. They died instantly.

The next few weeks were a haze. In addition to the funeral, the new Minister was on his way and needed the Manse. I knew I had to leave. As a Presbyterian Minister Dad didn't have any money, but the Church would take care of my College education. My financial situation wasn't good. Everyone was nice and some genuinely wanted to help. I was 20 and wasn't a minor. Several families offered to "take me in," but Frank and Ronnie really wanted me to stay with them.

All of the Wilson's appeared at the funeral, shocking some of the town-folks. Ronnie and Frank were pallbearers. Mom and Dad were heroes in a way to the Wilsons. Ronnie was the only star in the family tree and the Wilsons attributed his success to my parents. I hadn't been back to any of the parties in Wilson's Hollow, but several apparently had fond memories of me and thought I was a nice kid. The church wanted me out of the Manse. They said the new minister needed to move. I was homeless.

I put our furniture in storage and moved in with Frank and Ronnie for the summer. It gave me some breathing space before returning to college. As before, it was as if I had walked into a new world. It was a friendly and quiet world. I spent a week or so catching my breath. Frank and Ronnie were helpful, but never pushy. Ronnie was almost finished at the Community College and was to start a job as an Electrician's Apprentice in a month, so he had some time off. We fished and played as if we were still kids for the last time.

Oddly, I wasn't interested in sex. I guess when the world falls apart in one afternoon, you have too many things to think about. They were all big things and sex wasn't high on my list. However, since I was

20, sex had a natural tendency to rise. Frank still didn't wear many clothes around the house, nor did Ronnie. They were inspirational.

Buster came by to give me his condolences. He had been away and hadn't heard of the accident until he returned home. He showed up after dinner and we all talked on the porch. His Mom had died young too, so he seemed to be genuinely concerned. I found myself thinking of how good his cock head felt in my ass. It was hot and everyone was near naked. A big Buick drove up and a big bearded man got out.

"Bobby! Is that you?" the man in the car cried. I didn't know who he was. I said "yes" and must have sounded uncertain.

"Finally, I found you," he said. "I'm your Uncle Gus!" It didn't ring a bell at first, and then I remembered Mom's only brother, Gus. He lived in California and was never mentioned. As he got closer, he got better looking. He was a "Grizzly Adams" type, with an impressive blond beard and bright blue eyes. He was dressed as a businessman. "I'm sorry. I didn't find out until yesterday and I flew here immediately." He wanted to know all of what had happened, so I told him.

It was a hot night and the Wilson's were all but naked. This didn't bother Uncle Gus at all. They filled in details of my story. They knew all about the truck and the truck driver. He was a good man. An elderly couple pulled on the road in front of the driver, caused him to swerve and loose control.

"Have we ever met?" I asked. Gus laughed.

"Sort of, you were four the last time I saw you. Your mother and I were close, but your father and I were like oil and water," he replied. "I got a good job in Oregon and we just drifted apart. She was beautiful." The conversation flowed easily. He was a Professor of Anthropology and was interested in folkways and I guess you couldn't get any more folk than the Wilsons.

Frank suggested, we all might wet our whistles and Gus offered to help him get drinks. I was wondering what Gus wanted. I wondered if he was planning to take me away, or was just trying to pay his respects. Ronnie, Buster and I chatted on the porch. It seemed to take a good long while to get the booze.

I got up and went into the kitchen. From the front door, I saw Uncle Gus sucking Frank. Frank saw me and waved me closer.

"You and your Uncle share some of the same interests!" Frank said. Gus got up.

"Sorry, I got carried away," he said, looking embarrassed. I smiled.

"I've been carried away like that a few times myself," I replied. "We're all good friends here."

"And we mean real good friends!" Ronnie said as he entered the house. "We Wilsons are a close family and we stay close," Frank was getting undressed. Gus watched and unbuttoned his shirt. With that, Ronnie started to strip. I followed suit.

"Buster, come on in," Ronnie yelled. "We're going to have some fun."

From that point on, it was all sex. Gus looked like a Nordic god. He was 6-4, 240 pounds of toned muscle and covered in curly blond-red hair. His cock poked out from a forest of hair and nestled between huge low hanging balls. He was beautiful. He looked too good to be real.

Ronnie got on his knees and swallowed Gus' cock. I liked Ronnie, but he wasn't handsome. He sucked the cock as if it were the Holy Grail. About a minute later, I realized my Uncle was a sex pig. He loved it and wasn't afraid for everyone to know. He bent over to suck Frank, while Ronnie sucked him. He made sure his ass was wide open. It was hairy, pink and open for business. Buster poked his finger in it first. Gus moaned. Buster worked it in and rammed the prostate. Gus growled in appreciation. Buster finally coated his cock in oil and shoved it in the opening. Uncle Gus groaned in appreciation.

There was nothing Gus didn't like and no cock he wasn't interested in. We all moved from the kitchen to the bedroom, so we had more room to play. Gus told Frank, he liked to fuck and asked for a recommendation.

"Well my boy, Ronnie, likes it, but if you want a real good time, Bobby's the one for you," Frank said.

"Are you game Bobby?" Gus asked. I nodded

Ronnie had worked Gus' cock up. It's a real beauty. It was impressive, seven or eight inches long and torpedo shaped. Of course, to a Wilson it was the most natural thing in the world for an uncle to screw his nephew.

"Ronnie worked so hard," Gus said, "I'd like to give him a reward."

"Don't worry. Given his druthers, Ronnie likes his Daddy's meat. I'll take care of my boy," Frank said. "You give Bobby a spin."

I was on the bed and Uncle Gus probed my ass with his fingers. He went straight for my prostate and I almost fainted, it felt so good.

"You're right. He is a live one!" Gus said. He slowly removed his fingers and substituted his cock. It fit perfectly. If there ever was a cock custom made for an ass, it was Gus' cock and my ass. It was beautiful. Ronnie bent over me to suck my cock and get his meat within sucking distance of my mouth. I started sucking him, just as his father rammed his ass.

I tasted Ronnie's reaction. I remembered how excited he had been earlier, the first time his father visited his ass. He was just as excited. Ronnie, of course had a good view of Uncle Gus slowly massaging my ass with his cock. It was good for all of us.

"Sorry, there's no room for you, Buster," Frank said.

"Don't you guys worry about me? I don't mind sloppy seconds." Buster said. He had dropped down to where he could watch Ronnie, Gus and me. "Spread your legs some and I'd be glad to lick your balls, Gus." There was a little shifting. A few seconds later, I felt Buster's breath on my balls.

"That boy of yours seems to like being up close and personal with you," Gus said to Frank.

"It just keeps on getting better the more we do it," Frank said. "It never worked quite right for my Pa and me, but Ronnie took to it like a fish to water."

"Do you mind if I sample him some?"

"Not at all," Frank said. Gus pulled out of my ass to take Frank's place with Ronnie. Buster lost no time at all. His cock head was deep in my hole in a split second. It felt just as good as it had the first time. His large cock head traveled in my chute and worked its magic. Uncle Gus had been good too, but until now, I hadn't realized how different fucking could be. Gus' dick occupied all of me, Buster's cock head was a sex nut, poking into different parts of my sexual anatomy.

Buster didn't last long and Frank took his place. Ronnie must have liked watching his father's cock pound my ass. Ronnie was somewhat reserved, but his balls weren't reserved at all. They started pumping out pre cum with any sexual stimulation. Watching his Father fuck me, while my Uncle screwed him put his ooze making apparatus into overdrive. He popped.

We had a chain reaction orgasm. Each guy's ejaculation induced an orgasm in his partner. We were done in a minute or two, but no one wanted to move. No one wanted it to stop. We finally pulled apart and Frank went to get the drinks he had offered while we were on the porch.

It was dark, now so we went to the porch and sat down, still naked. We weren't on any road, so that wasn't a problem. "Bobby, I came here to help you. I was afraid you were abandoned," Uncle Gus said. "It looks to me, as if all is well. I had no idea we shared the same sexual interests."

"I had no idea you were gay," I said. "Is that why you and Dad didn't get along?"

"That may have been a part of it," Gus said. "Your Dad was a good, but timid man. He didn't want to take any risks. He figured, if you did everything right and obeyed all the rules, no one would notice you and you would be fine. I'm the opposite. I'm a live life to the fullest kind of guy. I think he was afraid of me. I didn't know your Mom had cancer. Was your Dad able to deal with it?"

"Sort of, but not really," I replied.

"He once told me, bad things happen to people who don't obey the rules," Gus continued. "I was afraid they would never accept what was happening. I guessed he would try to pretend it wasn't happening." Uncle Gus must have known my Dad far better than I did. He was right on the money.

"I kind of felt that way when Ronnie's Mom died," Frank said. "She was real pretty and real nice. She never said a bad word about nobody. Everybody knows that Wilsons die in bar room brawls, or DWI accidents. I kept on thinking I was meant to die and God made a mistake, bad aim or something."

"There's nothing wrong with you Pa," Ronnie said. "Nothing at all."

"Bobby and his Mom and Dad are what saved us. No one here is educated. I can barely read," Frank said. "Ronnie's a smart kid, smart like his Mom, but no one here knew how to help him. How could I help him with his biology homework, when I can't even spell biology? Sometimes things work out, just dumb luck."

"There is no such thing as dumb luck," Gus said. "You have to be smart enough to know luck when you see it."

Buster added an "Amen, Brother!"

"Changing the subject," Gus added, "was that incredibly good sex we just had here, or was it just me?" Everyone laughed.

"It seemed pretty good to me!" Buster said. "You ain't no virgin, are you?"

"I'm no virgin, but I've never been in anything so hot in my life!" Gus exclaimed. "Have you guys been practicing?"

"As a matter of fact, yes," Frank said. "Anyone from around here will tell you; we Wilsons are horny bastards and are willing to fuck anyone or anything we run into. I don't think they guess how true that is."

"Well, I'm willing to be adopted," Gus said.

"You really liked it?" Frank asked.

"Shit yes. You couldn't tell?"

"I did notice you weren't as shy as you might be," Frank said. "We don't get to do that often anymore; it used to be right regular."

"What used to be regular?" Gus asked.

"I guess you would call them parties, sex parties. When all the guys would get together one evening and fuck themselves cross-eyed," Buster said.

"Count me in!" Gus said.

"We don't let many strangers in, but you passed the entrance exam with flying colors. How long are you staying here?" Frank asked.

"I can stay a week, or two. Do you think you might have a party while I'm here?"

"I think I can pretty well guarantee it!" Frank said with some enthusiasm. "Where are you staying?"

"I'll get a room in a motel." Uncle Gus said.

"You're free to stay here, if you want," Frank said, "if you don't mind sharing a bed, that is, with me, or the boys."

"If you don't mind fucking your bed mate, I'm game," Gus said.

"It's a deal!" Frank replied.

Chapter 8

Uncle Gus spent the night at Ronnie's house in bed with Frank, Ronnie's Dad. We were in the next bedroom and at the end of the night, they had gotten to know each other really well. We heard it all.

When we got up, Gus was deep dicking Frank. Gus called us in and asked Ronnie and me to spell him some. Usually Frank wasn't that into bottoming, but Gus must have made him aware of the vast potential for pleasure. I replaced Gus and Frank's ass was hot and trembling. Frank's cock was rock hard and there was a puddle of precum on his gut, you could have floated a sailboat on.

"Damn!" I said. "You're hot!" Frank nodded. "Ronnie, you need to feel this!" Ronnie replaced me in his father's ass. Frank was leaking buckets, but the precum turned into a flood as soon as Ronnie got deep. Ronnie was moaning.

Gus watched approvingly. "I tried to teach him how to enjoy a dick in his hole. It looks like I succeeded!" He got on the bed and straddled Frank, opening his ass wide. "Open me up a little and guide it in, Bobby. An erection that good is too good to waste!" I worked my finger into Uncle

Gus' hole. It was warm and wet. Then I held Frank's cock and positioned it at Gus' ass hole as Gus sat back. The dick was coated in precum, so it didn't need any lubricant. The cock head vanished in Gus' pink hole, poking the rosebud into the dark recess.

Gus leaned forward and Frank's cock head popped out. Gus eased back again. On the third try, the entire cock slid deep into Gus' ass. Only the balls showed. Frank, Gus and Ronnie moaned at the same time.

It was hard to believe three well-hung men's genitals could be so compact. With Ronnie in Frank's ass and Frank in Gus, their cocks must have been pumping within an inch of each other's organs. They all loved it. Ronnie suddenly pulled out and shot his load on Gus' back. The milky sperm dribbled down. I guess the warm cum inspired Gus. He spurted all over Frank's gut and chest. Frank must have shot in Gus' ass. When he finally pulled out, he was still dribbling cum.

"Shit, if that isn't the best way to start the day with a bang, I don't know what is!" Frank said.

"You've got that right, Dad," Ronnie said.

"Damn, I'm going to be late for work," Frank said. "Can you boys fend for yourselves for breakfast?" We said sure. We all showered and had breakfast. Uncle Gus wanted to visit my parents' graves, so we went to the cemetery. All of the funeral flowers were gone; it looked bare.

"Do you have a monument yet?" Uncle Gus asked.

"Not yet. Money is kind of tight, so they told me to hold off until later," I said. "The Church said they might do something later."

"What in hell is wrong with the Church? I'll take care of that," Gus said, "both the monument and the tight money." We spent the next few hours selecting the monument. After lunch, we drove by my old house. There was a rental van there and a single man unloading it. Some of the furniture was way too big for him. Gus stopped and we got out.

We introduced ourselves.

"I'm Reverend Tom Washborne. I was so sorry to hear about your parent's death," he said. "This must have been an ordeal for you. We wanted to move a month or two later, but the Church said, they needed us here now." Washborne was in his late 30's, about six feet tall and looked as if he jogged. He had a close-cropped brown beard.

Ronnie and I helped move some pieces, while Gus and Tom talked. The Church had told me, the new Minister had to move now, so I was a bit puzzled when he said they wanted to move later. Getting out of the house had been a real problem for me. Most of the people in the Church were very nice, but several Elders were standoffish. I had been so preoccupied by my Mom's health problems; I wondered if I had missed something.

Tom Washborne seemed nice and he sure got along well with Gus. Ronnie and Gus moved some of the bigger pieces of furniture. Tom and I did boxes. An hour later, two men from the Church came and joined in. Tom's wife had a job she had to stay with for two more months at their old house with some of the furniture.

One of the men, Mr. Jones, was an old friend of my Father. I asked him about the new Minister's arrival date. He blushed. He said it was a long story that reflected badly on the church.

"We fought it, but Freddy Randall usually gets his way in the end," he said. Mr. Randall had been the bane of my Father's existence. He was a mean spirited, penny-pinching miser. He was one of those people who volunteer to do everything, not because his wants to, but so he will be owed enough by enough people to eventually run the place.

Mr. Jones told me Randall wanted my Father out, because they weren't getting full service from him. Dad was too preoccupied by Mom. It all made sense to me. Dad always said the great curse of Presbyterians was politeness. They were never rude and never wanted a scene. Randall had no problem with either. He could ride roughshod over the other members of the congregation. He also felt my friendship with the Wilsons, was unacceptable. They weren't the kind of people with whom a Minister's family should be associated.

It got late and several other members of the congregation showed up, so we went back home. We stopped at a supermarket to get some food. Gus said he would cook. Anytime Frank didn't cook was a blessing.

Ronnie heard the conversation with Mr. Jones and was riled. "I'd like to shoot that bastard. Mean ass hole!" Uncle Gus said the man wasn't worth jail time.

"I guess you are right about that," Ronnie agreed. Frank got back from work and brought Johnny and Joey with him. Johnny didn't exactly drool when he saw Gus for the first time, but he was close. Joey just stared in awe. Gus bought a lot of food and he asked Joey and Johnny to stay for dinner with us. They were more than willing.

Gus was a great cook and dinner was good. He also had some beer. It made the occasion more festive. It was a hot night and everyone was down to the minimum amount of clothes you could wear and not be technically naked. That suited everyone. Scooter and Charley dropped in just as dinner finished. They had a few beers before they got to the house and were in a real good mood already. They lived out of town and had a 45-minute drive. I wondered if Frank had called them to meet Gus. It turned out Buster called them. They were properly impressed.

I saw Gus looking at the three brothers, Frank, Joey and Johnny and I think I saw him drool a bit. Later, I found out he liked beefy, hairy men. Wilson's Hollow was the place for him.

"I forgot to get a dessert, guys," Gus said. "It might be too fattening anyway. It looks as if you watch your figures." Everyone laughed.

"Some banana cream is all I want," Joey said. "Even a small shot of it can be real satisfying."

"You must be a mind reader," Gus said. "Do you boys pitch or catch?"

"Are you talking sucking or fucking?" Joey asked.

"Why in hell are you asking that, Daddy?" Scooter asked. "There ain't nothing you haven't done and liked." Everyone burst out laughing. "You either did it to me, or I did it to you."

"Quiet. You might shock our guest," Joey said. "He might not be as open about cock play as we are."

"Don't worry about that. I'm open enough," Gus said. "Frank, Ronnie and Bobby can vouch for me. I know you men like to keep it in the family. Ronnie had a nice time with his Daddy last night. I have to admit it turned me on. Actually it turned me on big time."

"That's nothing special here, but keeping it in the family is fun," Johnny said. "You don't need to dress up!"

"Since when have we dressed up for anything?" Frank said. "Pulling up our zippers is formal wear for us." There was more laughter.

"I don't know about you, but I think we're all over dressed," Gus said. You could feel the sexual tension in the room. There was also a sense of relief. No one needed anymore convincing to get naked, or to start sucking.

It was confused at first. No one was trampled in the rush to get to Gus's cock, but it was close. Eventually he settled down with Johnny while Frank screwed Charlie and Joey massaged Scooter's prostate with his beer-can cock. Ronnie and I mostly watched.

Gus was in Johnny's ass in no time flat, so I got on the floor and sucked Johnny's oozer. Ronnie tried to slip in Gus' back door. He couldn't do that, so he rubbed his cock in the ass crack. The geometry of the positions wasn't right, but where there's a will there's a way. Gus worked Johnny to the floor and bent him over so Johnny could suck me. Gus then got in a position, so he could open his ass wider and let Ronnie in.

Gus liked the feel of Ronnie's cock as it rammed him in time with Gus' own ramming of Johnny. Gus was good about letting you know what was good and what was hot. It is lucky I like precum a lot. I could have drowned in Johnny's that night. I had sucked him before but then he had nothing like what he was drooling now.

Joey was deep dicking Scooter who was very happy.

"Damn, that's a thick one, Scooter. Do you have any trouble with it?" Gus asked.

"Nothing that ain't worth the effort. Daddy likes it tight," Scooter answered.

"Frank told me you have a beautiful ass," Gus continued, "Soft as silk and quivering."

"Are you going to try my ass out later tonight?" Scooter asked.

"Would you like that?"

"Shit, yes!" Scooter answered. "If we have the time, I'll fuck every ass in this room," Gus said. "On one condition though. I only give, if I can take. If you promise to leave your seed in my ass, I'll do the same for you." Just then, Joey popped his load and moaned in ecstasy as he filled Scooter's ass. Johnny's precum turned into cum, as he heard his brother's moan during his climax.

Gus knew how to make friends.

The first time I played with the Wilsons, Frank said the man sex was mostly blowing off steam for the Wilsons, a substitute for sex with women. He did admit he had a warm spot for Scooter and Charlie. In the week that Uncle Gus was there, I realized most of them just plain liked sex with men.

Gus was about as handsome a man as I had ever seen if you like your men masculine. He was a man's man, unaffected and fun. Uncle Gus was also a sex pig, a beautiful sex pig. He was handsome, muscular, masculine and always in-heat. He told me he liked men and he liked cock. He wasn't romantic; he was fun. He loved sex and loved to give his partners as good a time as he could.

I liked him. The Wilson men clearly loved him. He was everything they liked in a man. I'm not sure if any of them expected to bed a man as good looking as Gus. In their defense, the Wilson's had masculine down pat. They were 100% huntin' and fishin' red necks. They had cocks that oozed at the drop of a hat and were available for recreational use. You could also say they were unaffected, natural men. No one put on airs.

The Wilsons and Clansies weren't pretty at all. Ronnie was good looking, if you liked his type, the rest looked odd. They loved Gus.

Oddly, Uncle Gus liked them.

"This place is a fucking candy store!" he told me before he returned home. We were talking during one of the few times we were alone. Usually there were several Wilsons nearby, drooling. "I've never found so many men who were hot and ready to screw in one place in my life."

"You're complaining?" I asked.

"Shit no," he answered. "I feel as if I have died and gone to heaven. I've been to the South Sea Islands and never run into guys with as few hang ups about sex. This is an anthropologist's dream! If I wrote a paper, or a book about his, I could replace Margaret Meade."

"You aren't going to write about them? Are you?" I didn't think the Wilsons would like that at all.

"Quite frankly, I want to keep them all for myself. Exposure would destroy them," he said seriously. "They are the most exotic tribe of men I've ever encountered. If anyone found out about them, they'd be wiped

out. If they were in the Amazon and were inaccessible, you might be able
to publish something and not destroy them. Next door to the East Coast
Megalopolis, it's impossible."

"I think this sort of thing must have happened in early man. In
a small isolated tribe, incest is the only option, if the tribe is to survive,"
Gus said. "The Wilsons had a problem with mental retardation and birth
defects and solved it by institutionalizing homosexual sex. In antiquity,
other tribes abducted women from other tribes, like the Rape of the Sabine
Women. Large scale raiding parties are rare in modern America and the
Wilsons found another way."

"I never thought of it like that."

"It's clever. As long as they keep it in Wilson's Hollow, all is
well. They get to enjoy themselves and avoid the unwanted pregnancy
problem," Gus said.

"I've been thinking they must have a warm spot for man-sex
anyway." I observed.

"I know they do," he said. "You don't get this far into man sex
without a preference for it. The sex is hot and heavy, no holes barred. It
seems to me this is all male bonding, not incest in the traditional definition.
The recreational and fellowship aspects seem to dominate the sexual
aspects. At least until the orgasm!" Gus laughed. "They have no hang
ups, they aren't doing anything wrong as far as they can see it. It's like a
fraternal lodge meeting, except, fraternal in the original sense."

"I can't see the Elk's doing this!" I added. Gus burst out laughing.

"You've got that right!" Gus replied. "They'd have much better
membership if they did."

Gus didn't fuck everyone in the house that night after all. The
Wilsons wanted to do it right with a good, old-fashioned orgy. They had
struck sexual gold and wanted to share it with their family members. It
was the week before the 4th-of-July, so there was a long weekend. That
night they planned the party and decided to make it a camping event,
Friday night and all day Saturday and to invite only those with a genuine
enthusiasm for man sex.

I had never noted anything but enthusiasm in the men, but Joey
had definite thoughts on it. Some men had moved away. They decided

to invite Coach and Dave Anders and one or two other men who I didn't know.

Chapter 9

We had a few days to spare before the weekend. Ronnie's job started, so Gus and I went on some long, site seeing drives. He was unfamiliar with Virginia and he loved it. He had been to Tidewater Virginia's with its flat landscape, but had not been in the Valley or the Blue Ridge. One day we were leaving town when his rental car began to act up. We made it to Buck and Buster's tire shop when the car conked out. It was dead as a doornail.

Buck and Buster were nice guys anyway, but they went out of their way to help. We got a free tow to a repair shop and repairs were underway in half hour. Unfortunately, they needed a part sent in from Roanoke. It would be noon the next day before the car could be on the road.

Tom Washborne, the new Presbyterian Minister, was there getting a State sticker. He offered to take us home. Buck and Buster looked downright disappointed when we left with him. Until I met Gus, I wouldn't have believed a cock magnet existed. Somewhere between Gus' cock head and ass hole, something attracted Gay men. If they were within a hundred feet of him, within a day or two there would be genital contact.

I never would have guessed in a million years, Rev. Tom liked cock. He seemed like such a straight arrow. I also don't know how he realized Gus and I were into it too. As we drove, Tom asked me about Wilson's Hollow.

"One of the Elders told me, it's a den of iniquity." Tom said. "I have to admit, that statement did nothing to decrease its appeal in my eyes."

"You like dens of inequity?" Gus asked.

"It gives me a chance to do some heavy duty salvation work," he said. We were silent. "Hey guys, lighten up. It's a joke. Actually, I am interested in what members of my congregation classify as dens, or sin for that matter. This Elder hired me because I don't smoke or drink. That's all personal preference, rather than because it's sinful."

"I sure hope you have some vices," Gus said. "I have some I'm mighty partial too." He was smiling as he said this.

"As a matter of fact, I think Uncle Gus and I share the same vices," I added. "It must be genetic. We just met for the first time a few days ago."

"It's funny what some people classify as sinful," Tom said. "The Bible says nothing about drinking, smoking and damn little about sex. It's very clear about avarice, cheating and treating your neighbors like dirt. Somehow, this doesn't seem to penetrate the minds of some so called, 'Christians'. Some things are genetic. I think sex drive and sex preferences seem to be inborn. I'm not sure preaching at it will make any difference."

We got to Ronnie and Frank's house. Tom still was talking, so I asked him in. This seemed to be what he wanted. He entered the house and looked around.

"This doesn't seem to fit my vision of a den of iniquity. It looks like a plain old house to me," Tom said. Gus laughed.

"I wouldn't bet the farm on that!" he said, still laughing. "We all share the same vices. It may not be a house of virtue, but it sure is a happy house." Tom looked at us and was silent for half a minute.

"Wouldn't it be curious if we all shared the same vice?" the minister said. We looked at him and he looked down. He was wearing loose fitting pants and boxers. He was clearly getting a hard on. Gus smiled.

"I bet we do share the same vice. And I'll tell you one thing, we're always willing to have done unto us what we do to others," Gus said. "I all but insist on it." Tom looked at me.

"Bobby's kind of young." he said.

"Bobby is a full fledged member of the club. You don't need to worry about him," Gus said. "Bobby and his friends here have been teaching me a few things. And I'm no shrinking violet when it comes to man sex."

"I'm no shrinking violet myself," Tom said. Gus was already stripping, so we went to the bedroom.

Tom was a surprise naked. He was lean and muscular like a jogger with an even dusting of brown hair on his chest and a trail connecting it to his pubic bush. His cock stuck straight out and was a good eight to nine inches and almost as thick as his wrists. It was so large in proportion to his body it almost looked like he would tip over,

"Are you a fucker or sucker?" Gus asked.

"I like it all," Tom said. "You?"

"Never found anything I didn't like!" Gus said.

I said, "Amen!"

There wasn't anything Tom didn't like either. Ronnie came home while Tom was fucking me doggy style and Gus was rear-ending him. That didn't bother Tom at all. Ronnie joined in, as did Frank when he came back from work. Tom was a first rate top, forceful, but considerate. He didn't want to hurt you with his donkey dong, but you knew he would eventually get the whole thing in.

Tom's dick wasn't a perfect fit for me, but I sure knew there was some big meat in my ass. I kept on wiggling my ass to see if I could get more comfortable. He was thrusting, alternating deep and shallow penetrations. After Gus shot his load in Tom's ass, Tom pulled out, flipped me on my back and went at it again. It was on his tenth or twelfth thrust when it clicked.

I felt overwhelmed with sensation. I wanted his cock to be twice as big and go twice as deep. I wanted him to fuck me for the rest of my life. I suddenly wanted to cry at the prospect Tom would eventually shoot and pull his cock from my hole. My ass constricted and tried to capture his cock and keep it lodged deep in my insides.

"Damn! You really got him going!" Gus said as he watched. "Ronnie, Frank, watch this. You don't get to see this every day."

"Shit, I'm shooting!" Tom cried. Sperm emerged from his fucker with such force, I actually felt it spurting in my ass. After a few volleys, Tom pulled out and sprayed me and all the bystanders with cum. He shot an unbelievable amount of man seed. It took me a second to realize I shot off too.

Ronnie let me finish, and then began to lick my cock, while Frank licked up the cream on my chest. I could hardly breathe. It was that good. I could hear Gus talking to Tom. They sounded far away.

"How long does it take you to reload?" Gus asked.

"Thirty minutes usually," Tom answered. "I'm really turned on today, so it may be faster."

"I'd love to take a ride." Gus said.

"Let me warn you, the second shot can be a long time coming," Tom said. "I get real hard fast, but it takes a while to build up a good head of steam."

"You've made a study of this?" Frank asked. "Is it what they teach you at Theological School?" Tom laughed.

"After hours only!" he said. "I bet you know exactly how long it takes to shoot a second load?"

"It kind of depends on the inspiration for me," Frank said.

"Fifteen minutes for me, tops!" Ronnie added. "But I'm not much of a bottom, compared to Bobby."

"You have no trouble taking me?" Frank said.

"You're different Daddy," Ronnie replied. "You're family."

"You're kidding?" Tom asked.

"You're kidding about what?" Ronnie asked.

"Your Dad fucks you?"

"You're in Wilson's Hollow. They have different rules here," Gus said.

"You're the first horse hung Preacher man we've run into, who fucks like a rabbit," Frank said with a sly grin on his face. Frank reached over and stroked Tom's cock. It was hard as a rock again. "You may be shocked, but you're turned on too." He coaxed some precum from the minister's dick and coated the already bloated cock head with it. Tom smiled and looked a bit embarrassed.

"You're right, I could fuck a horse," he said.

"I'm next in line!" Gus said. He rolled on his back and hooked his legs with his arms, so his ass hole would be easily accessible. Tom moved into position and coated his cock with lubricant.

"You guys really fuck each other?" Tom said incredulously. He was nosing his cock head into Gus' wide-open hole. He was just popping the head though the sphincter and out again. "You don't mind if I play with your hole for a while, do you?" Tom asked Gus. Gus moaned in answer.

"Do you mind if I get an up close and personal look?" Ronnie asked. He moved into cock sucking distance of Gus' meat and started licking the cock, while he watched Tom's cock play with Gus' ass hole. Ronnie was spreading his legs and I knew what that meant. Ronnie wasn't a natural bottom; he usually protected his ass and kept his buns tight. He only relaxed when he wanted something in his ass bad.

"Would you like to watch me fuck my boy?" Frank asked. "I usually only do it at family events, but, being you are so interested and a guest and all." He paused. Ronnie was feverishly licking Gus' meat and deep throating between licks. "When Ronnie gets this way, nothing but his Dad's cock will do the trick." Ronnie had pulled his legs up under his body and then spread his knees, so his ass was wide open.

Frank was wrong about one thing. His cock wasn't the only one that could do the trick. Mine could and did. I loved Ronnie when he did that. He only opened up for guys he trusted and loved. That was his Dad and me. I loved the feel of a cock in my ass. Ronnie opened up to please those he loved.

"Does Ronnie want it?" Tom asked. Ronnie couldn't say anything because his mouth was full with Gus' cock. He smiled at Tom.

"I remember how nice it was the first night my Daddy did me," Frank said. "I was the runt of the litter. Jesse, Joey and Johnny had all been taking it for a year or two." I lubricated Frank's cock. He pushed the head into Ronnie's ass in imitation of Tom's fucking technique. "They told me it was good and they had been playing with me for years, but I was convinced Daddy would never screw me. He finally asked me to the hunting lodge, but everyone had either screwed me or let me suck them, but Daddy. I was on the floor taking Grandpa when Daddy came up behind me and slipped in." By now, Frank's cock was halfway in Ronnie's ass and Ronnie was in heaven.

"My Daddy said, "Shit, it's smooth as silk," as he went in all the way the first thrust," Frank continued, "At least 12 guys had shot off in my hole that night already, so I was real open. He bent over me and stroked my cock. Daddy said, "Shit, you've got one hell of a cunt plug!" with that, Daddy shot his load."

"It turns out Daddy liked them big and he realized he had a lot of home grown entertainment in his own back yard," Frank continued. "Now Tom, see what I'm doing now?" Frank was pulsing his cock about three fourths of the way up Ronnie's love chute. "If you get the chance, rub him there, it drives him crazy." I knew the spot. It was one of those places that felt so good it almost hurt.

Ronnie gave the impression to me that he and Frank got it on only at parties. Frank knew an awful lot more about Ronnie's love chute than you would learn in a few encounters a year. Ronnie looked completely relaxed as he sucked Gus and Frank massaged his innards.

"Did you get to play with your Daddy much?" Tom asked. He was getting real hot and bothered and it was hard for him to talk. He was at the point when the feelings in your cock are so strong you can't think any more.

"I sure did. He was built like Ronnie, but wasn't a natural born bottom. He liked them big and wanted them big, but it took some work before he could take it all," Frank continued," I was afraid Ronnie would be like him and my dick wouldn't fit. Ronnie is tight, but not too tight." Frank started to breath heavily. "You've done it again, Ronnie, I'm going to shoot."

"Pull it out Dad and show Tom your seed!" Ronnie asked. Frank did and seconds later, cum covered Ronnie's hairy back. That was enough to induce orgasms in Tom and Gus. Tom, Frank and Gus were wasted by now, but Ronnie and I were ready to go again. I took Tom and Ronnie eased into Gus' ass. They weren't enthusiastic at first, but were good sports. Tom had to get home, so we relaxed, had dinner and went to bed early.

Frank was very tired, so Gus slept with us. Ronnie's trip up Gus' love canal must have been real good. They spent the night coupled one way, or the other. I slept and sucked whatever cock was near whenever I rolled over. For a day that started with a broken down car, it had turned out really well.

Chapter 10

As I said, Gus was a cock magnet. Word of his attractiveness and unquenchable sexual appetite spread throughout the Hollow. We had planned to resume our site seeing trips through Virginia, but Wilsons and Clancies appeared at the door to say hello and see Gus. Johnny and a cousin named Eddie appeared the next day in the early afternoon. Eddie was a Clancie. He was red headed and about 6 feet-2, thin and put together like the Scarecrow in the Wizard of Oz. Eddie was 55, or so and you could all but see his cock hanging out of his cut off jeans.

Eddie almost drooled when he saw Gus. Gus was amused and intrigued. Gus was only wearing shorts and he rearranged himself to give Eddie a view of his balls. Eddie was a man of few words, but seemed to have a powerful itch in his cock, so he started stroking it.

We were on the side porch of Ronnie's house and couldn't be seen from the road, so Gus just dropped his shorts to give Eddie a complete view. Eddie almost passed out he was so excited. He swayed some, then dropped to his knees and started sucking Gus.

"You've got to forgive Eddie for lacking the social niceties. He's from deep inside the Hollow and doesn't mix with most of us. He says, we put on too many airs," Johnny said. "He doesn't get out much."

"Someone taught him all he needs to know about cock sucking!" Gus said. "Eddie, you're real good at what you're doing."

"I'm not sure I have ever encountered a group so devoted to man sex as you Wilsons," Gus said. "Here it's normal to play with your relatives. It's not kid's stuff, "you show me yours and I show you mine." It seems to be anal penetration every time, heavy duty man ramming."

"It's kind of strange; Eddie must have learned cock sucking in the Army. His part of the family was a bit lax in the hygiene department, even for Wilsons. Sucking cock was no walk through a rose garden, if you get my drift," Johnny explained. "When he came back from Nam, he had a taste for cock and he and his sons all like it. They swim regularly in the summer at least. His oldest, Donnie, calls summer the sucking season. Fucking is leftover from the old days. At least with fucking you don't need to smell the cheese."

"Oh, by the way, don't worry about talking to Eddie, he's deaf. A bomb blew up too close. He ain't as dumb as he looks, he just never learned to read lips," Johnnie continued. "Would you like to fuck him, Bobby? He loves to be fucked while sucking." I was embarrassed; I didn't want to fuck a man I barely knew.

"Why don't you?" I asked. "He knows you."

"Come to think of it, I don't mind if I do!" Johnny said as he disappeared into the house, emerging a little later with a bottle of lube. He dropped his shorts, kicked them away and squirted some lube on his cock. Eddie glanced up from his cock sucking duties and spread his ass, so his hole was easily accessible.

Johnny popped in the hole without fanfare. Eddie didn't miss a second in his worship of Gus' cock.

"It's hard to believe, but Eddie has the best fuck tunnel I've ever felt," Johnny said. "He looks skinny and scrawny, but his chute is smooth as silk." Johnny moaned in pleasure. "Bobby, get naked and try him out! Eddie would love it." I was turned on by then, so I stripped and lubricated myself. Johnny pulled out and I went in.

Eddie grasped my cock with his ass muscles and massaged my cock as I fucked him. Eddie was good. He appeared to be all but still, but his ass was churning and quivering. He seemed to have some muscles most guys didn't have in their ass.

"Shit, Bobby! You've got him up! It's real hard to get Eddie hard, but you've done it," said Johnny after I'd been pounding Eddie for a while. "Have you ever had a 12 incher up yours before?" he asked.

"Hey! I might like it!" Gus said. "I'm into new experiences." Johnny pried Eddie from Gus' cock and Gus got on his back and rolled up his legs and held them behind his arms. The pink hole beckoned to Eddie. Eddie might have been a confirmed cock sucker, but he sure had an interest in fucking too. He greased up and worked his way in.

At first I though he had an incredibly long, but thin cock. I later realized that its 12" length gave the illusion of being slender. It was a good inch and a half in diameter. Eddie went slowly until the first eight inches were in, then he rammed the rest.

"Shit! You've hit something new!" Gus exclaimed. Three stokes of Eddie's cock later and Gus sprayed his chest with semen. Poor Eddie looked disappointed; he clearly wanted a longer fuck session. Gus was winded. The afternoon's exercise left us soaked, so we all went inside and showered. Gus and Johnny showered first, and then I showered with Eddie. He has softened up some, so it was only hanging six or seven inches.

He sucked me and I had to admit Gus was right, Eddie was a first rate sucker. He worked a finger into my ass too. He was licking my precum and he knew that by pressing my prostate he could increase the flow. He got up and I went to suck him, but he said no.

"I want to save it for the party," he said. "My boys and I will give you a good fucking then," he added. I must have looked uneasy about that. "Don't worry kid. You'll love it; we're real careful and nice. You won't believe there's so much man seed in you when you finally shoot."

We went in the other room. Gus was walking stiffly.

"You've got a real telephone pole there!" Gus said. "Taking your cock was a challenge. Sorry I popped so soon." Eddie was deaf, but sensed what Gus said. I guess everyone he fucked said about the same thing.

"You took it real well," Eddie said. "I love to watch a man shoot. You had a good load. If Randy, my son was here, he'd have been in cum-licker's heaven."

"Is Randy back in town from the Marines?" Johnny asked.

"Yep, he got leave two nights ago, got here last night. Robbie and Rex got very excited seeing him again. It had been a might quiet at the house," Eddie said. "They wanted to pop their loads for Randy, but I told them all to wait. It will be more fun at the party."

"I forgot Randy liked it so much," Johnny said. He was real excited. "Do your younger boys have the same interests?"

"Those boys were doing the fancy dance on Randy's love pole long before I had a chance to try them on for size," Eddie said. "When Robbie took the whole thing the first time, I knew he'd been practicing." Eddie didn't always catch all of the conversations. He always responded, but not always to the question asked. "It turned out good, though. It took a while for Randy to like it. He wanted his dad's cock in his ass bad, but it wasn't a perfect fit. Robbie was nice and open. So was Rex."

"You always took care of your own," Johnny said. "Joey did Wilburt. We brothers are so close there really isn't much cock difference between us. We've traded off. Wilburt was so screwed up; it was a relief to find out a good cock could solve his problems."

"My kids are good boys," Eddie said with pride. "My Dad wasn't too good at it, so I was real glad they liked cock play. It sure makes the long nights shorter. There's nothing we've tried that wasn't fun."

"Did your boys fuck you too?" asked Gus.

"Sure. Strange, that's the most fun sometimes," Eddie mused. "Randy got them to save up for a whole week once. They all rear loaded me, and then Randy gave my hole a tongue bath. You can't believe how long that boy's tongue is! He got his fill of cum that night!" The conversation continued for a while, but Johnny and Eddie had to go, so Gus and I were alone until Frank and Ronnie returned from work.

Just before he left, Eddie asked, if he could bring his boys by the afternoon of the party. "They've never been to one before and I'd like for them to know some of the guys there."

Gus said, of course it was fine. They left and Gus and I started talking.

"You know, I thought the man sex was a once in a while thing at first," I said to Gus. "It was only for special occasions. Frank said some of them were really into it; others could take it or leave it. Since you've been here, it seems to me a lot more are into it than aren't. You seem to have brought out the cock hound in the Wilson genes."

"Quite frankly, they've brought out the cock slut in me," replied Gus. "I've never done anything like this before, except for a few hours in a bath house in L.A. years ago. I hate to say it, but I could get used to it. In L.A., New York or even Amsterdam, this all would be perverse beyond imagining. Here, it's plain old family fun, no hang-ups, no worries. It's all just a nice way to spend an evening as far as they are concerned."

"It sure ain't Mayberry!" I said. Gus laughed. "Are you as excited by this as I am?"

"I sure am. If anything, I'm more excited. I've been in heat since I got here."

"It's not that I'm just a know nothing teenager?" I asked. "I thought this might be the way things were in some places."

Gus laughed and said, "Not even close! I don't know of any place in the world where people act like the Wilsons. Don't worry about your inexperience. I didn't fuck a man until I was in my 20s and didn't get fucked until thirty. I'm not into kids, but you're no kid. You give it like a man and you take it like a man. The first time I screwed you, you laid back, opened up and let me in. You were open to the experience. After three thrusts, I knew we were meant to be fuck buddies. You are my sister's kid, but we were meant to fuck!"

Frank and Ronnie got home and we told them about Eddie's visit.

"He's got a long one!" Frank said. "I tried his cock once, but it was as if he was cock punching me deep in my ass; it was too long for me."

"That's the way it felt to me," Gus said. "It wasn't exactly painful, but it was on the edge."

"Eddie's never been to one of the parties, has he?" Ronnie asked.

"Not in years," Frank said. "He gets along well with his brood. Real well."

"Like you and me?"

"It's a lot closer than you and me. It's sort of like Scooter, Charlie and me," Frank said. Ronnie knew what that meant. I cooked dinner that night and we all went to bed early. The parties tended to go on for hours, so it was nice to have a restful night the day before. I slept with Ronnie and Gus slept with Frank.

"Dad told me some guys from the deep Hollow are coming to the party," Ronnie said, "They are real back woodsmen."

"You mean you guys are the sophisticated Wilsons?" I said. Ronnie giggled as he grabbed my cock.

"Yep! Believe it or not, there are some real Hillbilly types in our family. Dad says they're a bit crude. They heard about Gus and want to see for themselves," said Ronnie. "Dad's making them come here for a dip in the swimming hole before they go to the hunting camp. They don't take baths regular, but they will swim. They like Daddy and will do what he says. "

"Why is that?" I asked.

"It's a strange story."

"Ronnie, what in hell in the Hollow isn't a strange story?"

"I guess you're right about that," Ronnie conceded. "This all happened before I was born, so it's just what I've heard. The Deep Hollow Wilsons had a leader, a chieftain called Major. He was the meanest bastard in the group. You may have noticed that we have a warm spot for cock; well Major didn't share that liking. He fucked, of course, but he liked to hurt. It was a power thing. He liked young boys specially and they all hated him."

"He sounds like a nasty character," I said.

"He was mean and nasty. Well Major came to one of the get togethers. He rammed Joey good and hurt him. Dad got mad and figured, turnabout is fair play. Dad was young, but strong then, got Major on the floor, and forced his horse dick in Major's ass. Major squealed like a stuck pig, they said."

"Did that teach him a lesson?" I asked.

"Yes, but not the lesson Dad expected." Ronnie said. "Daddy hit the 100% fun spot on his second time in. Major had a virgin ass and had no idea how good a cock could feel ramming him deep. He thought he had died and gone to heaven. Major couldn't get enough of it; they fucked for an hour or more. Major still couldn't get enough. Daddy pumped for another ten minutes and shot his load deep in Major's ass. Major popped and went limp, dead as a doornail. He had a heart attack and died."

"Shit! What happened next?" I asked.

"Well, Daddy told me it got stranger," Ronnie continued. "They took the body home and buried it. The Deep Hollow Wilson's keep everything in the family. Daddy went to the burial. Everyone seemed pleased that Major died with a smile on his face and everyone was even happier the bastard was dead."

"They had a get together afterwards and they wanted Daddy to go with the men folk to their hunting cabin. Daddy didn't want to do this, but he felt real bad he had killed Major, even if he was a bastard," continued Ronnie. "He figured they wanted some revenge and it was rightfully their due."

"He was wrong. As I said, Major was a real bastard. They wanted to try out Daddy's cock. That and drink his cum," Ronnie explained. "His sons wanted to feel what their Daddy felt just before he croaked. They loved it too. Eventually they had him screw some of the women folk, so they could have their own, home-grown version of his dick."

"Ronnie, when you said this was a strange story, you were sure right about that," I said. "It can't be true." Ronnie laughed.

"Well, Daddy swears most of it's true. He always made them take a bath before he would fuck them and it seems the tradition dies hard," Ronnie added. "Major's been dead for a good thirty years and they still have fond memories. When Daddy married, he stopped servicing the Deep Hollow Wilsons except once and a while. Dad told me, they still keep to themselves mostly. They only come to our parties every few years. Dad doesn't know any of the current generation."

"I guess we will know soon enough," I said. We fell asleep without shooting. Frank said we should save up for the next day.

Chapter 11

Eddie and his brood and extended family arrived at Frank's house at noon. They came with a few extra cousins and an Uncle, or two. The minute I saw Reggie, I knew he was Frank's son. Except for their ages, they were almost carbon copies. Robbie looked like Eddie, his Father and Rex was a wild card. Rex was about my age, but almost pretty. He had curly, black hair, a clear complexion and beautiful pale blue eyes. In spite of his age, a thick mat of black hair covered his chest.

Uncle Royal looked like a Wilson, bear like. He was ten, or fifteen years younger than Eddie and Frank must have visited his wife. Royal's son, Royal Junior also looked a lot like Frank. The Dick of Death must have been in big demand all over the Hollow. The other Uncle, Festus, was a red haired, bear-like man and he was with a guy they called Cousin Lem.

We all went off to the pond for a swim. Uncle Joey showed up and came with us as did Ronnie and Frank. I commented on the mixed appearance of the group.

"Eddie's wife was a bit of a party girl," Joey said. "She was always up for a good time. Eddie had a friend, a postman name Willy Wilsonholm. Eddie loaned him his wife a few times and that is where Rex came from."

"Does that bother Eddie?" I asked.

"Not at all; Willy died in an automobile accident," Joey said. "Eddie likes having a reminder of his old friend. I didn't know Frank had popped Royal's woman." I wondered if the old Wilson taste for family play applied to the deep woods Wilsons. Gus came up to me and whispered. "Which one of his sons will Frank fuck first?" he asked. "Want to make any guesses?"

I shook my head.

We arrived at the pond. We stripped and jumped in the water quickly. After a nice swim, the men got out of the water one by one. Royal, Festus, Robbie and Joey gravitated toward Gus. Royal Junior, Reggie and Ronnie stayed near Frank, their father. Festus and Lem were with Rex and me. Rex sat next to me.

Rex was slim and muscular with a treasure trail connecting his hairy chest with his thick bush. His cock was a good, thin seven incher and was half-erect.

"Have you been to one of these parties before?" he asked, Rex had a strong mountain accent. "Are they fun?"

"They're fun if you like man sex," I said.

"Hot damn! I sure like that," Rex exclaimed. He got closer. "Do they suck or fuck?" he whispered.

"Both."

"Hot double damn! I like it in my ass, but never been fucked by anyone other than my brothers and Daddy," he said. "Are you family?"

"Nope."

"Do you mind havin' a stranger's cock up your shit hole?" he whispered and got even closer. "I've never been with a stranger before." He was fully erect. I realized he was excited and a bit scared at the prospect of a new experience.

"Don't worry. Ninety percent of the men are your kin. The others are really nice," I said. "If you like man sex, you'll have a good time."

"I get kind of crazy when I get fucked," Rex said. "I don't want to make a fool of myself."

"You won't be the only one who likes it and you sure won't be the only one to get crazy," I said. I stroked his cock and a bead of precum emerged.

"Daddy says my cock milk is real good," Rex said. "Would you like to try it?" I said, "Sure." He was right. His cock oozed a thick, creamy liquid. I deep throated him and he twitched. Rex's cock reacted to every movement of my mouth and lick of my tongue. Rex really liked sex and responded as if his cock was a joystick.

"Hey guys!" Someone yelled. I looked up and it was Frank. "We all got matching dicks!" Frank was in the middle, flanked by Reggie and Royal Junior. They were displaying their hard and perfectly matched dicks. They were all horse hung.

"Damn, you boys make a pretty sight!" Eddie said. "Frank, you sure solved the meat shortage in the Hollow. We got the length, but you got the heft. You must have the most potent cum in the family."

"I didn't know I hit the bull's eye so often," Eddie said. Uncle Johnny wandered up.

"You boys are getting started a bit early!" he said. "Save some cum for the party." He stripped and jumped in the water. His arrival defused the sexual atmosphere. I had thought we would start the party early. Instead, we all went into the water again. The afternoon was getting hotter and the water felt good. Gus was in the water next to me talking with Eddie and Royal, trying to find out more about their sons.

"It was hard to keep Momma happy," Eddie said. "She was always in heat. It was nice to take a night off sometimes. She liked Frank and Willy. So did I. I figured, if I liked their cocks in my ass, Momma might as well get to try them out. I knew she wasn't going to leave me, so a little fun for her was fine."

"Real open minded of you," Gus said. "Are you open minded, Royal?"

"Not at first. My old woman said she wanted to tryout something other than my beer can. She said, I was thick enough, but didn't go deep enough to drive her crazy. I know Frank was family, but I still wasn't sure," the bear like man said. "But, once Junior was born, he grew on me. My other kids are girls and nothing but trouble. Royal Junior has been a blessing."

"It's funny though," Eddie continued, "I think I liked Frank and Willy's dicks more than she did. I couldn't believe how good Frank's horse dick was in my ass. He had killed that ass hole, Major, with it. I didn't have one minute of problem with his donkey dong. I was kind of proud of that. Momma said he was almost too big for her. Frank said she was really tight and he popped right off. That's funny, because Willy, said it took him forever to shoot."

"I watched Frank kill Major," Royal said. "I had never seen Major so happy as when Frank was pounding him."

"Did you get to sample his cock?" I asked. Royal put his arm around me.

"Actually, I fucked him," Royal said. "I was mad as hell my old lady was knocked up and was going to fuck him to get even. Damn if I didn't have the best screw of my life! I ended up spending the night with him and must have shot ten or twelve loads in his ass." Royal had worked a finger in my ass. I felt his cock under the water. It was a true beer can, thick and short.

"Royal Junior looks like Frank and has the same ass hole," Royal said. "He must have been almost 20 before I popped him, but he wanted it when he was twelve. I like for a guy to open up the door for me. I don't like to knock it down. The Major did me when I was a kid and it was awful. Ever since getting fucked by the Major, I wanted him grown so it would fit good."

"What if he didn't want you?" I asked. "

"You win some and you lose some," Royal said. "I'm a big boy. I'm not going to cry if I don't get everything I want."

"Willy is Rex's father?" Gus asked, turning the conversation back to Eddie. "What was Willy like?" Eddie didn't hear Gus correctly and it took some time for him to understand Gus' question.

"Willy was my best friend. He was almost pretty, sweet natured and fun," Eddie said. "Until I met him it never occurred to me to screw around with someone who wasn't kin. He delivered the mail one day when no one else was home and I jumped him. Actually, he may have jumped me. We knew we wanted to get in each other's britches the first time we met. He wasn't really into women much; it took a lot of talking to get him to bed Momma."

"She was interested?" Gus asked. Eddie laughed.

"Momma was always interested. Some people thought she was slutty. I thought she just liked a good time. She didn't mean anything by it. I knew she like man meat before we hooked up. She always hopped in bed with me after she'd been playing. Cum lubed her up real good and I could get deeper. She loved that," Eddie continued.

"Willy wasn't very good at bitch poking. As I said, he wasn't really interested. Willy died two days later and I can't tell you how happy I was when I discovered Momma was knocked up with Willy's boy. I never missed anyone so much in my life as I missed Willy."

It was getting late and we went back to Frank and Ronnie's house for dinner. We went off to the Hunt Club around eight. Scooter and Charlie, Joey's sons were there with Wilbert. Wilbert was Uncle Johnny's son. They were all naked. The State Trooper, Dave Anders and Coach Allen arrived with us, as did Tom, the Minister.

Five minutes later, Uncles Johnny and Joey arrived with two younger guys, Cousins Fred and Bill. They were slightly older than me. I didn't know who they were related to. Coach Allen went over to them. They must have been on one of his teams. He was naked and when they stripped, they already were fully erect. They looked embarrassed, but Coach talked to them. I remembered the talk he gave me at the first party I had attended.

The last men to arrive were the twins, Buck and Buster. They walked through the door naked, identical except Buck, who wore a gold necklace. Rex stayed near me, but he sure glowed when he saw the twins. They both looked like Bluto and that must have turned him on. Gus must have felt the same way. He joined them.

Rex, Gus, Buster and Buck formed a huddle, talking quietly. They all were semi erect and while they were just getting acquainted, there was no hiding the attraction. Tom, the Minister came over and joined them.

When you are naked and excited, there is no way for a man to hide his interest. They made no effort to conceal their erections.

Coach Allen and Dave Anders were talking to Fred and Bill. Apparently, Anders had discovered them sucking truckers at a rest stop. The attendant had called him to arrest them. Anders found they were Wilsons and took them to Johnny. They were from a branch of the family, which had found religion and were violently anti sex. Johnny and Joey decided they needed a better outlet for their sex drive than a rest stop.

Frank was in the middle of a cluster of his sons. They were having a good-natured dispute as to who would fuck whom first. The Wilson compulsion to have sex with your sons and father left them with a problem. Of the three, Ronnie, Reggie and Royal Junior, only Ronnie had been with Frank. They all wanted to try him on for size. Reggie and Royal Junior seemed fixated on Frank's cock.

Scooter and Charlie were with Eddie, Royal and Cousin Lem. They usually played with Frank, but had left with his newly discovered sons. The lighting was dim and I wondered who would be the first to get the ball rolling.

Uncle Joey came by and handed me a tube of K-Y. "These are old fashioned Wilsons here," he said. "Lubricate everyone's ass. No dry fucks tonight. The deep woods men like that and it's the hard way. Everyone is going to be ready." He told me to do Coach Allen's group. Coach saw me coming and understood what I was supposed to do. He bent over and opened his ass.

Fred and Bill looked shocked and their cocks grew even harder. Both Coach and Dave, the Trooper, liked being fingered and weren't afraid who knew just how much they liked it. By the time I got to Fred and Bill, the boys knew it was all right to like it. Fred was scrawny and there was more cock than man when he was hard. Bill still had some baby fat, but he would outgrow that soon enough.

"Have you men ever done any fucking?" Dave asked, while I was working the lube into Bill's ass.

"Not really," Fred answered. "I sure have thought about it a lot."

"I fucked a truck driver once," Bill said. "It was okay. I'm not sure I was doing it right." I had moved on to Fred. He winced as my finger poked through his sphincter, but relaxed as soon as I was in. I rammed his prostate.

"Shit, what in hell was that?" he asked. I kept the pressure on the organ and poor Fred was in ecstasy.

"Let me make a deal with you boys," Coach said. "If you want, Dave and I can give you a lesson in butt sex. It may hurt some at first and it may be a bit messy, but I can all but guarantee, you'll have the best night of your life."

"If you think the finger is good, just wait until you get a man cock up there," Dave added. The boys didn't need any convincing. I moved on to another group.

Buck and Buster had been watching Coach and so the twins bent over together and I lubricated both.

"You can use more than one finger, if you want," Buck said. "I've got a big hole." I was on my knees with two fingers up each ass. From this position, I could apply pressure to their prostates and the twins were moaning. This was too much for Rex; he joined me on his knees and started to suck both men, frantically moving from cock to cock.

Gus told me to lubricate him, when I pulled my hand out of Buck's ass, Gus took a squirt of lubricant and coated his cock. He then poked it in Buck's ass. Buck sighed in relief. Tom watched this and substituted his cock for my fingers in Buster's love chute. Buster moaned as the preacher's cock entered him. I lubricated Tom and Gus' asses and then they all went at it hot and heavy. The twins were kissing and supporting each other while Tom and Gus gave them a deep dick fucking. Rex was in the middle, on the floor, sucking the cock drool from the twins.

"Holy shit!" someone moaned. It was Royal Junior taking Frank's cock for the first time. When I looked closer in the dim light, I saw Junior was in Ronnie's ass. Ronnie was obviously enjoying his half brother's version of his father's cock.

As I watched, Reggie rear-ended Frank. It was clear, not only did their cocks match; their asses were identical too. I had never seen a four man fuck before. I joined them and got on the floor so I could do some ball licking. I knew Frank liked this and wondered if his sons did too. The four men were cock to ass, twitching rather than thrusting. If they tried bigger thrusts, the cock might slip out. I had a feeling none of them wanted that. I couldn't work my way in between them, but the view was remarkable. Three cocks in a row lodged in quivering holes.

They were all big, so there were three or four inches of cock visible, except for Royal Junior who was deep in Ronnie's ass. Scooter called me to come over to him, so I left Frank and his brood slowly group fucking.

I went to Scooter's group next. Lem volunteered to go first. He wanted several fingers too. I did two, then three. He was breathing hard, but wanted more. Royal came over to me.

"Try to get the whole thing in," he said.

"My whole hand?"

"Yep, Lem likes that." I tried four fingers. That still wasn't enough for Lem; he wanted something big in his ass. My hand was dripping with lube and I pushed one more time. It popped in and his ass clamped tight on my wrist. Lem was finally satisfied. He had my entire hand up his ass. I had no idea what to do.

"Just turn it real slow and push a little deeper," Royal said. "It's real tender in there, but Lem loves it. Lem was out of it with his eyes rolled back in his head. After awhile I pulled my hand out and Robbie took my place. Robbie was Eddie's middle son and the only one who looked like his dad. I went out to the back and washed off. Royal followed me.

"Eddie told me you were a real nice boy," he said. "Festus and I ain't no lookers, but we kind of hoped you'd play with us." He paused. "We like to fuck. We like it a lot."

"I don't mind, but why not fuck with your kin," I asked. It seemed to me the Wilsons' had no hang-ups and weren't too picky either. Festus and Royal weren't lookers, but they weren't awful either.

"Were the bottom of the barrel as far as the family is concerned," Royal said. "They'll screw us, but never let us fuck. Festus emerged from the shadows. He was hairy and thick, a typical short, fat man.

"I'm really a nice guy, just ugly," Festus said. He had a bad stutter. "I've never fucked a pretty boy like you. Eddie said you were real nice," Festus added. I wasn't interested, but I felt a bit sorry for them. I reached over and stroked Festus' meat. It must have been three inches in diameter, but was short.

"Let's go back inside and see what happens," I said. We went in.

Everyone was occupied and going at it heavy now. We were in a corner and I started to suck cock. I discovered several things in the next few minutes. Festus wasn't fat at all; he was solid muscle. Underneath his thick coat of curly, red hair, he had a pair of monster balls. His cock head had a wide piss slit that let my tongue get deep into his cum chute.

I switched to Royal and found he was the opposite, with a thin, long cock, much thinner than Eddie's meat. They were brothers, but were all but different physically. Both were appreciative and enthusiastic. Royal and I got into the 69 position. His cock slid way down my throat, but was thin, so I could suck and breathe at the same time.

Royal and I broke apart and I told Festus to get on the floor, so I could take a seat. I had the tube of K-Y with me and coated the thick member. I straddled him and sat back, peeling the foreskin as the cock slid into my ass. I don't know exactly what happened. Looking back, I think the thickest part of his cock head must have occupied the spot my prostate liked to occupy. The smallest movement sent me to the moon. I just twitched and oozed buckets of precum.

His cock and my ass hole were exactly the same width and I was skewered on his meat with no way to escape the unrelenting pressure on my prostate. I couldn't think it was so good. Royal lifted me off his brother's cock and slipped his probe in. His mushroom head sat on the end of his almost painfully thin shaft. After Festus stretched me to the limit, I couldn't feel Royal's shaft at all, only the head. It felt as if there was a living thing wandering around my rectum.

It was exciting and pleasurable, but relaxing, after my time on Festus' cock. Gus had wandered over to see how I was doing. He had finished with Buster and Buck.

"You sure had a good time on that cock," Gus said.

"Unbelievable," I said. "You should try it out, it was a wild ride." Much to my surprise Gus did. He sat on Festus' cock and it had the same effect on him as it did on me.

"Holy Shit!" Gus exclaimed. "You don't look like much, Festus, but you sure got it where it counts." Festus blushed.

I don't want to sound like Mother Theresa, but Gus and I gave Festus the best sex of his life. It was Beauty and the Beast with Gus grinding on Festus' butt plug. Our ass holes had done a good deed and Festus looked like a junkyard dog who had just found a loving family.

Chapter 12

A big round table occupied the middle of the room. At earlier parties, it was covered with snacks and drinks. They were on side tables this time, so the round table was clear.

"Hey Guys!" Uncle Johnny yelled. "Since we have so many guys from the Deep Hollow, we thought it might be nice to do an old fashioned ring fuck. Gramps used to love it, but we haven't done it in years.

"Is it like a daisy chain," Scooter asked.

"Combination daisy chain and musical chairs I guess is the best way to describe it," Johnny said.

"With a little King of the Mountain thrown in," Joe added.

"You want to do it that way?" Johnny asked his brother.

"Sure, we got company, we want them to have some fun too," Joey answered. Johnny nodded.

"Now guys, this ain't the kind of game they play at ladies' bridge clubs," Johnny said. There was a snicker.

"How do you play it?" Ronnie asked.

"Hold your horses, I'll get to that," Joey said. "Let me tell you. It is not for the faint hearted and involves a lot of fucking. Once it gets going, there isn't any choice. If you have a cock here you don't want in your ass, you'd better sit this one out. If there is a cock that doesn't fit, you need to sit it out. Fred and Bill, you're new to this. You can watch. This is not the place to learn the ins and outs of ass sex."

"Awe," the two boys said simultaneously. They sounded disappointed. Coach put his arm around them.

"Don't worry boys. Dave and I will have you broken in by the time of the next party." Coach said. "You'll be pros by then."

It clearly was a gang-bang sort of thing. I wondered if I wanted to do that.

"It starts with the young guys on the table, with their Dads doing the fucking." Johnny explained. "Anyone who wants to try another ass, touches the shoulder of the guy next to him and the men rotate. Any man who shoots, drops out and anyone in the room can replace him in the ring. Any son who shoots is replaced by his dad."

"Who wins?" Charlie asked.

"Everybody," Joey said. "It's over when it's all Dad's on the table, or when everyone's shot off so much they can't get hard again. Since we have some extra sons here, we'll let them replace their bothers and when we run through the sons we'll switch to Dads."

"Wilburt, you get over here and get on that table," Johnny said. "Open that shit hole of yours wide, we've got some fucking to do. Frank, you start with Ronnie. Eddie, you can pop Robbie, if he wants to play." Scooter, Joey's son, was already on the table, he and Charlie had flipped a coin. "Gus and Bobby, are you game?" I wasn't sure. Gus looked at me.

"It sounds really strange," I whispered to him. "Shit, I'd love to do it if you start me off," Gus broke into a wide smile.

"We're game, Johnny." he said.

"Royal, you can do Royal Junior? Now Tom, Rex here is sort of a wild card. I guess you are unattached too, want to try it?" Johnny asked. Johnny was no fool. He had watched Rex and Tom look each other over and the two men jumped at the opportunity. "Buck and Buster, Festus is left. Willing to take a ride?"

"No problem," Buck said. There were eight guys on the table with a ring of eight men ready to fuck them. Buster, Charlie, Reggie, Lem, and Coach Anders' quartet were watching.

Wilburt was next to me on one side, Rex on the other. I could feel Rex's heart beating. He was really excited at the prospect of Tom's cock in his ass. Wilburt was excited too. Usually Joey fucked him. I think he was excited at having his Dad behind the thrusting cock.

"Legs up on the shoulders. We've got tons of lube, slick up the meat and grease the oven door," Joey instructed. "You bottom boys, hold hands. You need to support each other, or you will bang your heads together as the fucking gets heavier. Rex and Wilburt held my hand.

"Gramps thought it was nicest if we all go in together," Johnny said. "He said, it made a pretty picture."

"Too late for me," Royal said. There was a roar of laughter.

"Well just pull it out and pretend!" Joey said when the laughter subsided. "Is everyone ready? Gramps said, you don't need to go deep on the first thrust, if the boy doesn't like it. As long as your cock head is on the inside of the ass ring, it counts as a fuck. All together now. One. Two. Three!"

Gus' cock slipped deep on the first thrust. It was a good as always. Johnny went deep into his son Wilburt's ass. Wilburt squeezed my hand tight. He didn't relax until his Dad's third or fourth thrust. Rex held tight as Tom's head popped through the ring. Tom stopped there and then pressed slowly. He had big meat and there was a long way to go before he was fully lodged. When Tom was half way in, Rex moaned and let go of my hand. All was well there.

The entire game was artificial and stupid until the fucking started. Direct cock-to-prostate connections break down inhibitions quickly and having 16 men in heat, really warm up the atmosphere.

"Damn it, I'm shooting," Ronnie cried. There was a commotion on the other side of the table as Reggie replaced his half brother on Frank's cock. Reggie sighed in satisfaction as his Dad's cock went deep. Royal popped too, and Buster took his place in Royal Junior's ass. Royal Junior seemed to like that a lot too.

Gus touched Johnny's shoulder and the fuckers rotated one person to the right.

Wilburt came alive when Gus poked deep. I had a feeling Johnny's cock didn't fit perfectly. Gus' did. Gus was handsome and Wilburt liked him. Tom's cock did a job on me. I had taken it before and it was good, but I must have loosened up some. Gus' cock could have done a lot of loosening, I guess. It was big and went deep. I couldn't think of anything, other than Tom's donkey dong in my ass. I heard Scooter cry out as he climaxed. I realized Frank would have been in his ass by that time, after the rotation.

Charlie replaced him and got to feel Frank's cock too. Charlie, Scooter and Frank were real close and it was nice they got to get off together.

Reggie popped and left the table. I think it was Festus who made him shoot. Frank was the first of the Dads to be fucked, since he had to replace Reggie on the table top. Joey, his brother, fucked Frank first, so they had a good time talking about old times.

"Reggie sure shot a nice load," Joey said. "He reminds me of the loads you shot. Remember the time you got Gramps in the mouth?"

"I don't think you can aim a cock and I know you can't guess how far you will shoot," Frank said. "It was purely an accident. Gramps sure liked it. He thought I did a special favor for him. By the way, Joey, if you want to rev it up a notch, it wouldn't bother me a bit. I could use some pump priming."

"How often did you boys do this?" Tom asked. I couldn't see him, but I think he was fucking Buck by them. He sounded a bit winded.

"Fuck parties or ring fucks?" Joey asked.

"Ring fucks." Tom replied. The men rotated again. Somehow, Royal Junior was next in my ass. I don't know if he had shot off and recovered quickly, or had just decided to top for a while. He had Frank's cock, but with a more aggressive attitude.

"Not more than every three or four years, as I recall," Frank said. "They usually did it after a lull in the parties, when everyone had built up a good head of steam. Gramps came up with the idea, so we had a good one after his funeral."

"That's my idea of a funeral," Gus said. "Everyone promises to get naked and fuck someone you love after the service." He was breathing heavily. He was pounding Wilburt's ass. Wilburt began spraying everyone with his seed as Gus fucked him to an orgasm.

Johnny replaced him on the table, so he got to sample some of Gus' fucking technique.

Dave, the State Trooper, replaced Royal and thus was the next man in Rex's ass. Rex was one happy guy. By now, I lost track of who was fucking whom. The night turned into a haze of pleasure and stimulation. Everyone was sweating like pigs and covered in lube, cum and precum. The room smelled of man sex. Buster replaced Tom in my ass. Buster and I had a real good time. He shot a big load and then got Buck to replace him.

That may not have been the way the rules were, but the twins liked sharing the same ass, especially after the other twin had cum in it. Buck came quickly and was replaced by Bill, one of the new kids. He popped after three strokes and Fred replaced him.

Fred was the scrawny, well-hung one and he was good. I think his cock fell in love with my ass. With three men's cum in my love tunnel, there was no resistance and his tool slipped in to the hilt. Bill had been too excited to notice much. Fred liked where he was and took his time. Fred was a lover, not a fucker and that combined with his big tool, made for a real nice time.

Fred couldn't have had much fucking experience, but he was a natural. He watched my reactions and when I twitched, he made a note of that and went back to do it again. By this time, we had been going at it for 45 minutes and the energy level was diminishing. It was less frantic. Everyone was pumping slowly and it was peaceful.

Frank, Joey, Eddie, Gus, Royal and Johnny were being fucked on the table. Rex, Robbie and I were the only ones of the original bottoms who hadn't shot off. Most had recovered from their first orgasm and had come back to life as tops. Wilburt spent a good fifteen minutes in his Dad's ass. I think that was unexpectedly good for both of them. They usually didn't get along that well, but they sure were friendly as Johnny shot a massive load.

By now, there was no effort at rotation. Everyone just fucked whoever they felt like. Ronnie came over and slipped into Rex's ass. Ronnie is my best friend and not as well hung as some of the guys. Rex didn't look too excited, until Ronnie's beer can rammed his prostate head on. Twenty hard thrusts later and all the sperm Rex had been saving all night, burst out and sprayed everyone within ten feet.

Fred continued to slowly pump me. Reggie plowed Frank and Eddie was squirming on Robbie's dick. We were the only ones still at it. It was nice, but I wasn't sure if it would ever end.

Gus came by with a bottle of poppers. He gave me a snort and then gave it to Fred. Fred had never done poppers before and wasn't sure what they were, for a few seconds. Gus went over to Eddie, then Frank. A minute later there was cum flying everywhere. Some must have hit the ceiling

Everyone calmed down a lot after that, especially me. I was bushed. I was ready to sleep, so I crawled up on a bunk bed in the corner and dozed off. I figured it was midnight, or early in the morning by then. I woke up an hour or so later and the party was still going strong.

It was a little before 11:00 and everyone got their second wind. Rex, Fred and Bill came over with Dave.

"The boys here want to try their hand at bottoming," Dave said. "I thought maybe you and Rex could give them pointers. After the session earlier tonight, I was thinking a nice quiet time would be good."

"It just came natural to me," Rex said. "I'd been watching Reggie and Robbie screw for years and wanted to be included in the fun."

"Did it hurt?" Bill asked.

"I guess it did, sort of," Rex said. "Robbie was easy, but Reggie was bigger. It hurt some, but it also felt better. Daddy caught us and that ended it for a long while."

"He got mad at you?" Fred asked.

"No, he got mad at Reggie. He had been playing with them for a while and told them to tell him when I was ripe. He kind of wanted to be the first cock in my ass. He ended up being the third. It all worked out good in the end. Daddy was the first guy I ever fucked. Dad loved that. I look a lot like Dad's old friend Willy. Dad said my cock was exactly like

Willy's. He got screwed by his best friend, eighteen years after his friend died. It was a miracle, Daddy said."

Rex had been stroking his cock the whole time and had a good boner by now. Dave had been doing the same. I was thicker than they were and it seemed to me they would be a better first screw than me.

"I didn't have any trouble the first time. Junior opened me up and Frank finished the job," I said. "Dave added the finishing touches later that night."

"Who is Junior?" Bill asked.

"He's Frank's nephew. I had never met him before."

"Was it odd to have a stranger's cock in your ass?" Bill asked.

"The strange thing was to have Frank's cock in my hole," I said. "I didn't believe it would all fit." Dave was lubricating the boy's asses. Bill seemed to like that a lot. He was squirming and moaning some.

"Get on your hands and knees and we can do a little test," Dave told Bill. Bill got in the position. Dave got behind him, with his cock placed in the center of Bill's hole. "I'm just going to apply some pressure. You can fight it, or let me in. It's just to get you use to having a cock at your hole." Dave continued. He pressed. Bill groaned. Dave's cock vanished without a trace.

"Damn, that's good!" Bill said. Bill was on his hands and knees, but he dropped his torso to the ground, so his ass was as open as it could be.

Fred looked at me.

"I'm kind of big for a first fuck." I said.

"I'd like to try it." Fred said.

Chapter 13

I was in the corner of the room with the two boys, both desperate to feel more cocks in their asses. The Coach and his friends had taken care of the initial deflowering. They wanted more.

I am not much into young guys, but we had a good time. I like the top and bottom and don't mind switch hitting. It was quiet, slow and easy going. It wasn't as much fucking, as sex play. Cocks slipped into an ass or two, but it was relaxed and pleasant.

The relaxed atmosphere made it a lot easier for the boys. Fred and Bill liked man sex. They wanted to be part of the group, but the low-key fuck session let them relax. As they relaxed, their asses relaxed too. Ronnie joined me and our cocks slipped in their holes without effort. I got deep into Bill's ass. You could almost see a light bulb go off in Bill's mind, when my cock was fully lodged in his ass. I was the first to hit his prostate and fucking made sense to him.

I took Fred's cock and enjoyed it more than I would have thought. There was also more cock than I had realized. Fred was thin and a bit scrawny. His cock looked big, but I thought that was in comparison to his body. It didn't just look big. It was huge.

It was lucky the men who had fucked me earlier had opened me up. It was also lucky I hadn't realize it was as big as it was. Fred eased it in. It was thick and stretched me. I took that well. When he began to shove it in, it felt better. The shock was when the massive dong kept on penetrating deeper and deeper. The last four inches were a chore.

Fred knew he was big and was nice and gentle. It was clear he wanted to get his entire cock in my ass and wasn't gong to be deterred. He didn't need to pump, my whole ass was filled to the brim and there was nowhere else to go. It wasn't as pleasurable as the other big cocks, but the feelings were extremely intense and sexual. He left it in, just making little pulses. It began to feel good.

We had attracted a crowd, encouraging him and me to continue. Fred pulled his cock free of my ass, and then shoved it a bit less slowly than the first time.

"Shit! I don't believe that monster fits!" Ronnie said. Fred pulled out again. Buck coated Fred's cock with a new layer of lubricant. Fred went in for a third time. He was thrusting harder and faster now. He looked at me. He wanted the fuck me harder, but didn't want me to be hurt. I winked at him and he began to fuck me at full speed.

Fred didn't last long. He pulled out and sprayed the audience with cum. It was a spectacular series of ejaculations. The crowd applauded. I felt relieved. I was glad I had taken the cock, but wouldn't do it every day. I felt good to be free of the monster dick in my gut. Rex cuddled up to me.

"That was about as exciting as anything I have ever watched in my life," he whispered in my ear. He slipped down and sucked my cock. He knew my ass was getting back to it's normal diameter by the time Rex slipped his cock into the hole. He didn't fuck me, he massaged my prostate with his cock. It was beautiful. It felt wonderful.

I began to shoot. Fred was there and sucked me while I ejaculated. He told me it was the first time he ate cum. He wasn't into cum, but he felt he owed me. The party was coming to an end.

Coach Anders and Dave, the trooper came over to me before they left the party. "You are going off to school?" Anders asked.

"Yes, I leave the day after tomorrow. Gus is taking me to California for the rest of the summer and I will fly back for college."

"I'm having a little party at my cabin tomorrow. Would you and Gus like to come over?" he asked. "It will be tame compared to this, but you should be able to have some fun."

"Who will be there?"

"Well, I call it the "Graduation Exercise."" Coach said. "There are several other guys in the area who share my taste in men. Other Coaches, Scout Leaders, men like that. You know there are some kids like you that want man sex and would love to have it with their coach. I never mess around with kids on my team, or at school. Nothing but trouble there. I have enough kids trying to brown nose me without knowing I like cock."

"Well, after graduation, and after they turn 18, we get together. The Coaches and the kids meet for an "up close and personal" session," Anders continued.

"It might be embarrassing to run into some friends," I said.

"Remember, they will be just as embarrassed as you." Coach said, he was smiling. "You are off to college. You'll never see most of these guys again. No one knows who will show up. Usually we play with the guys from neighboring schools, not our own. That's not a hard and fast rule, but most guys are happy playing with a Coach, not his own Coach."

"Where is it? I have to talk to Gus about it." I asked.

"Don't worry about Gus, I've already talked to him." Coach said. "I gave him the directions."

I talked over my experiences in the Hollow with my Uncle Gus after the party. I was on my way to college and there wouldn't be much chance for the open sex as practiced in the Hollow, in even the most liberal college town. I guess it would be hard to visualize more sex in a single place than I experienced in Wilson's Hollow. My Uncle Gus seemed to think with the possible exception of some wild night in ancient Rome or Greece, the party at Wilson's Hollow was about as good as it got.

I don't think I had missed sucking a single cock and every cock in the Hollow spend some quality time in my ass.

"You sure enjoyed yourself," Gus said.

"You mean you didn't?" I replied. He smiled.

"I got my share. It's going to be odd, going back to the tame sexual practices of California." Gus said. "The Wilsons have this all down just right. Did you notice that no one got left out, no one got jealous? Stripping sex of its religious and romantic overtones, made it into purely recreational activity. That sure takes the stress off."

"Some guys were more enjoyable than others." I said.

"I know, but was the sex with the guys you really liked always as better then sex with guys you barely knew?"

"Not always. Ronnie's a good friend and the sex is good. Wilburt is just a guy and the sex is great." I replied. "It must have to do with his cock and my ass."

"Frank's cock does more to you, than it does for Ronnie. I can launch Ronnie to the moon whenever I want." Gus said.

"I hadn't noticed." I said. "Ronnie likes you that much?"

"Yes he does. You are open and receptive. Ronnie fights it some, it makes for a tighter fit and a more intense sexual experience," Gus said. "Once I get in, Ronnie gives up completely. He surrenders and opens as wide as any man I have ever screwed. You still maintained some control. Ronnie's mine!"

"Frank does that to me," I confessed. "And, you're right. Sex with Frank is great, but I'm a lot more attracted to Ronnie. Frank's cock isn't that pretty either. It's a magic wand in my ass."

"I think it's the cock and the way it is shaped and fits that makes the difference," Gus mused. "The cock head and the prostate are the most sexually wired parts of a guy's anatomy. We don't really know how they work exactly. Once you popped into the hole, your cock is blind. Ronnie's short stubby cock does a job on my prostate. I feel as if it rams it and stays there until I shoot. Ronnie just melts to my cock. We merge."

"I don't know exactly what Frank does. I can't think straight when he's in me." I said. "Frank's long, thick meaty and uncut. Anyone of those traits could be what does it."

"Maybe it just too hard to analyze sex," Uncle Gus said. "If I could explain it and write a book about it, I'd be a wealthy man. I'd love to write something about Wilson's Hollow, but I can't do it. It would destroy them. It has to remain our little secret."

"I'm not going to tell! I'm just glad I discovered sex now. Left to my own devices, I might have missed it entirely," I responded. "I'm good at it too. Are you sure you're supposed to feel guilt? I have liked every minute."

"You have had a baptism of fire," Gus said. "Although, I guess it would be more correctly a baptism of sperm. You're a trooper."

"How did you react to your first experiences with man sex?" I asked.

"Thinking back, I was so excited I hardly knew," he said. "I was in my late twenties. I had been successful with girls and had been fucking my way through college. A guy blew me once. That was good, but not exceptional."

"It became exceptional?" I asked.

"It sure did. I went to a convention in New York and ended up sharing a hotel room with a flaming fagot, florist. It was one of these reservation screw-ups. They had double booked the room and Kenny was there first. He was good enough to let me share it. Kenny was a flamboyant guy, so funny and outlandish you immediately liked him. He was tall and beautifully tanned with a big, Elvis style wig. He wore gold chains; Hawaiian shirts opened to his navel and had a hairy chest. He looked macho, but had a lisp so thick it turned English into another language."

"I got back from a banquet late and a bit drunk. We had a few more drinks and Kenny made me an offer that sounded good to me and my drunken state. I expected a simple blow-job. Kenny was the Michelangelo of cock suckers. I was his Sistine Chapel. I loved it. He just didn't stop, my cock had never felt so good."

"Eventually we were both naked and I tried sucking him. I felt it was the least I could do, given how good he had been to me," Uncle Gus said. "Kenny's cock was all man. I liked it. I liked it a lot. The hotel called the next morning and told me they had found a room. I said, I'd stay put. Kenny was pleased. I went to my meetings, but Kenny said, we would have a great time that night."

"He was right about that. I got back early that night. I wasn't drunk and went out to dinner with Kenny. He calmed down some and when we got back, he asked me if I would like to fuck him. I said what the hell. I'd been fucking cunts for years. Kenny's ass was a revelation. He was tight and must have had several extra muscles. He was the dream bottom. I had never been so appreciated. I loved it. Later that night he worked a finger into my ass and introduced me to my prostate."

"You discovered it is one of your favorite organs?" I said, laughing.

"It sure did. He fucked me before breakfast the next morning. He was big and I was tight, but I did realize there was potential. I was sitting on his cock, thinking it wasn't too bad and wasn't too exciting either, "Gus continued. "He must have had five inches in and three to go, when I went crazy. It was strange to be thirty years old and suddenly discover there is an entire world of sex I hadn't even dreamed about."

"Kenny was a master fucker too. I stayed an extra day and he filled in the gaps in my knowledge. I had heard guys talking about fucking and had no idea it was pleasurable. It always seemed degrading. I admit, having a guy shove his cock into your shit chute doesn't have much of a ring to it. Damn, I love it!"

"I had never totally surrendered before. I let Kenny do anything he wanted and I discovered it was as good as it gets. There was no attitude, no game playing, no one-upmanship. It was just two guys trying to see how much enjoyment they could have. The party last night was like that. All fun, no stress."

"And that is why you are here in rural Virginia and fucking and being fucked by a bunch of Hillbillies?"

"Yep, that's it." Gus said. "And loving every minute of it."

Johnny drove up to the house as we talked on the porch. Gus had a call and needed to call a friend in California. We went to Johnny's house and Gus made the call. Close friends in California had been a major car accident. Gus had to get back. We drove to Washington the next day and were in Los Angles that night.

My summer in Wilson's Hollow was over. I wanted to go back, but that wasn't possible for the next few years. I also missed the Coach's "Graduation Exercise". So I never found out what happened the next day.

Knowing the Coach's sexual tastes and drives, I guessed there would be a few very happy young men the next day.

.

PART TWO: RAPTURE GRANGE

This part of the story is told by Bobby's Uncle Gus.

Chapter 1

I spent the summer in Virginia, settling things for my nephew after the death of his parents. While there, I found he had fallen in with a remarkable group of mountain men who regularly got together for what could only be called male orgies. Hillbilly Hollow was a remarkable place. Settled by a single family and threatened by the genetic problems generated by intermarriage, the Wilsons used homosexual sex as an alternative sexual outlet.

They regarded incest as applying only to male-female sexual relations. Man-to-man sex was purely recreational, without any particular stigma. For them all sex had been a family affair for generations and the prospect of sex without the fear of pregnancy, birth defects, or retardation seemed positively virtuous.

I spent a good part of the summer there. While I can't vouch for the virtuous aspects of the arrangement, I can definitely state the recreational aspects were wonderful. I am a Professor of Anthropology and I had never encountered anything like it. It would have been great to write a paper on

Wilson's Hollow, but the publicity would have destroyed the family, not to mention getting most of the men sent to jail.

I did discuss the arrangement with one of my closest professional colleagues, Dr, William Baselstrode. He was fascinated. Bill and I were old friends, but only professionally. I was uneasy about telling him, but he understood the significance of the Wilson's approach. Here was a small group of people who regarded homosexual activity as a good, indeed desirable activity. He also understood the requirement to keep it quiet.

"You participated in the parties?" he asked.

"I sure did," I replied. "And, quite frankly, it wasn't purely from scholarly curiosity. The sex was unbelievable."

"The word around the Department was that you weren't inexperienced in the sex department," Bill said, smiling.

"The sex at Wilson's Hollow was as open, easy and as good as I had ever dreamed. Actually, it was a lot more than I had ever considered. My dreams were tame. It is such a unique arrangement." I said.

"Not quite unique," Bill said. "I know of one somewhat similar situation. It's a group, nearby, just over the mountains. It's religiously based."

"How did you find out about it?"

"It was a fluke, just like your encounter," Bill said. "I was traveling and my car broke down in Rapture on a Friday evening. The car couldn't be fixed until Monday, so I had the weekend to kill. There was one motel in town and there was a wedding, no room at the inn. I stayed in a tourist home. It would be a Bed and Breakfast today. The place was run by a middle-aged hippie, whose wife was away for the weekend."

"Sam, the hippie pothead, had a real informal dress code when his wife was gone. I was the only guest. The place wasn't air-conditioned and it was in the middle of a heat wave. Sam had a new hot tub and insisted I try it out. He was naked, so I got naked and jumped in. I am, what I guess you would call, a big boy. Sam seemed to like that a lot," Bill explained. "Did you know I'm gay?" he asked.

"No, but I never thought about it either. Everyone west of the Mississippi knows I'm gay," I said. Bill laughed.

"I'm a few years older than you, I never felt comfortable being that open," Bill said. "I never mix my professional life with my personal life, but I do admire your work for our Department. Anyway, returning to my story, Sam was a size queen of the first order and had no problem at all making me feel at home. Hell, I wish I had someone at home like Sam. Not the hippie or pothead part, just the cock sucking aspect. I'm pretty experienced myself and Sam and I really hit it off sexually. He said he was versatile and open to the possibilities. That understated the case."

"The next morning Sam told me, there was a meeting that afternoon I might like at the Grange Hall. I was skeptical about it, but he told me more about it. It was part fraternal organization and part sex club. At first, I thought it was a New Age, Earth Mother-fertility god thing. It wasn't."

"I was surprised he asked me to come. It seemed to be this defined secret society and I was a complete stranger. I asked him about it."

"Shit man, half of the entrance requirement is hanging between your legs, the other half you passed when you shoved that horse cock of yours up my love tunnel," Sam exclaimed. "Shit, I haven't been reamed like that in years. Damn, I've never been fucked so good before." He paused. "Don't worry one bit about the membership in the Grange. With your cock, you could become the Grand Master in a day or two."

"Well, quite frankly, I wasn't too sure of the whole thing, but I had nothing else to do, so I went along." The phone rang in Bill's office. It was a quick conversation.

"I have to go. The Dean needs me," Bill said.

"I need to hear the rest of the story!" I complained. He laughed.

"Don't worry, I'll fill you in on the rest. There's a meeting this weekend. Are you free?" he asked. "I know you meet all the necessary requirements of the group. You'd love it."

"I know I would like to, but my nephew, Bobby, is still with me."

"Is he the one who found Wilson's Hollow?" Bill asked.

"That's right."

"If he's game, bring him along. The Rapture Grange is nothing if not open minded," Bill replied. "How old is he?"

"He's 25 now. He was 20 or so when he discovered that Hollow in Virginia," I said. "I'll talk to Bobby and ask him if he wants to come along." The minute I said that, I knew what Bobby would say. He had no problem with the sex at Hillbilly Hollow; he'd have no problem with the Grange.

Friday afternoon the three of us were in Bill's car driving to Rapture. Bobby and Bill hit it off from the start. Bobby is polite and interested and has no problem talking with adults. It was a six-hour drive and as we began to approach Rapture, Bill began telling us the story of the Grange.

"Rapture was founded shortly after the Civil War by a group of unhappy Mormons. Women who created the group were deeply offended by the taste for multiple wives of the leadership of the Utah branch. They essentially told their husbands to leave with them or they would leave on their own. The group settled in the mountains of northern California and created a modestly prosperous farming community." Bill explained.

"The ladies were opposed to polygamy, but they also felt women should be in control of sexual agenda. Since they were the ones to get pregnant and would be the ones who might die in childbirth, they felt they should run the show," Bill continued. "This tended to leave the men high and dry for much of the time. This was just fine for the women and indeed, the fatality rates for mothers and children fell dramatically. But, there is a marked difference in the sex drives of women and men and there was unhappiness among the men."

"One of the founders of the community, Virgil Jackson found a solution. While reading the Bible and came across the story of David and Jonathan. He then pondered on the relationship between Jesus and the Beloved Disciple. It became obvious to Virgil that the two greatest figures in the Bible had loved men and this wasn't condemned."

"As a good Biblical scholar, Virgil was aware of the traditional Sodom and Gomorrah story. He studied it in detail and decided the problem wasn't with man-to-man sex; it was forced sex. He decided the main problem of sex in the Bible was with sex between unwilling partners," Bill continued. "Virgil compared David's love for Jonathan to that of another Old Testament Hero, Sampson. Virgil found David's love vastly superior to Sampson's destructive passion for Deliah."

"Virgil was a member of the local Grange."

"What's a Grange?" Bobby asked.

"Essentially it was a fraternal organization devoted to protecting and helping farmers. It was one of the great late 19th century institutions in America. It was originally called the Patrons of Husbandry," Bill explained. "While it referred to agricultural husbandry, Virgil took it in another way. At the meetings, he explained his new Biblical understanding. Apparently, there were some like-minded men in the group. Frankly, I guessed most of the men were so sex starved they were willing to try man-to-man sex as an alternative to the cold beds at home. Virgil proposed having some special "convocations" to deal with sexual needs."

"Did everyone join in?" I asked.

"Not all. You remember Virgil was deeply opposed to forced sex, but maybe a bit more than half of the men joined," Bill said. "That is how the Rapture Grange got its start. It had bi weekly meetings: one is of purely Grange type things; the other is for sex."

"It's a purely sexual meeting?" Bobby asked.

"Mostly," Bill replied, "but, I'm not sure it's only that. You need to experience it. I won't tell you anymore. I'd like to have your opinions about the group afterwards." We were on the edge of Rapture by then. There was quite a bit of new development on the edge of town. We passed by the McDonald's and NAPA Auto Parts stores and went into an older residential area. It was attractive, but not exceptional. That may have been good for the town, since it wasn't over run with tourists.

We drove up to a rambling house in a heavily overgrown yard. It was Sam's tourist home. In spite of the overgrown yard, the house itself was in good condition. Sam was tall and thin, bearded, balding and wearing an unbuttoned Hawaiian shirt.

"Hey, good to see you Bill, who are your friends?" he asked. "Looks like you found Grizzly Adams."

"You like?" Bill asked.

"Shit yes."

"This is Gus and his nephew Bobby. They are full-fledged members of the fraternity. Gus teaches with me at the College," Bill explained. "I figured they'd like the Grange meetings. Both are into man sex big time."

"You figured right. We could use some new meat. Come on in and get settled," Sam directed. "You're the only guests here, so join me in the hot tub when you freshen up."

We went to our rooms. It was a two-room suite, connected by a bathroom. The house was a bit rustic, but the bath was cutting-edge and up to date. Bobby and I took one room and Bill the other. I washed up. Bill came in the in the bath as I was finishing.

"When you're done, wrap yourself in a towel. That's the official hot tub attire. I'm heading down. I want to catch up on the local news," he said. "I'll meet you there." Bobby wanted to take a shower, so we arrived at the hot tub about fifteen minutes later. We wandered through the house and found the hot tub in the back yard. The yard was jungle-like, so overgrown the greenery completely hid the tub.

Sam and Bill were in the tub, a third man sat on the side with his back to us.

"Gus and Bobby, come on in!" Bill called. "Sam has a friend he wants you to meet, Virgil Jackson." He paused and then added, "Virgil Jackson IV." The man with his back to us rose and turned to greet us. He was tall, thin, balding, and had a luxuriant red beard. The beard merged with his chest hair. His gut was hairless except for a treasure trail to his pubic bush. His pubes were as thick and bushy as his beard. A long uncut, white snake hung from the bush. His balls hung low in his hairy ball sack. Virgil smiled. We shook hands and I dropped my towel as I got into the water.

Virgil checked me over and seemed to like what he saw. As Bobby got into the tub and sat on the edge, I noticed Virgil's cock jerked and grew a little as he checked out Bobby's cock. Bobby was 25, six feet and 160 pounds. He had not filled out yet, but his cock was man sized. He was cut with a big mushroom head, bisected by a wide slit.

"Sam said you were coming to the Grange meeting tomorrow," Virgil said.

"We're planning on it. Are you the admission committee for the Grange?" I asked. It was obvious to me he was checking us out.

"No, but quite frankly, if I was, you guys would have passed the entrance exam when you walked into the room," Virgil replied. "I don't want to sound crude, but Bill is as good a judge of man meat as anyone I've met, if he's brought you here, I know you're okay."

"Virgil, I thought you told me, I was the best judge of man cock in the town!" Sam said in a mock complaining tone.

"Well, you found Bill and Bill found Gus and Bobby, here," Virgil said. "That makes you a good judge in my book."

"You are a descendant of the founder of the Grange?" I asked Virgil. "Bill told me something of the history of the organization."

"Yep, Great-Great Grandson, or maybe Great-Great-Great Grandson. I'm the only direct descendant male left of the founding family who has stayed in the area. I do have some cousins and an uncle or two by marriage here, but I am the only direct descendant of Virgil."

"Are there many of the descendants of the original members in the organization now?" I asked.

"Not that many. As the community has grown, we have gotten members from the general population," Sam said. "We have some of the local leadership, like the Mayor, Fire Chief and a Judge as members. They fill up the roster."

"Classy group," Bobby commented.

"We got a lot of rank-and-file guys too," Sam said. "It's not a business men's club. It's pure fellowship and recreation; no shop talk at all. That's not permitted."

"Is that a rule?" I asked.

"It's one of them." Virgil said.

"What are the other rules?" Bobby asked. "I'd hate to embarrass myself at the first meeting I attend."

"Virgil's Grand Daddy wrote up some in the 1930s. There are in a minutes book," Sam said. "No one knows if they ever were officially adopted, but everyone acts as if they were."

"Rule one is privacy. The club and its activities are private between members and not for discussion outside the group.

"Rule two is membership is based on interest in man sex and no other aspect. Today it would be a non-discrimination rule, but at the time, it was written there were no residents here other than white men. They were apparently worried about poor verses rich and fat or skinny men.

They didn't want the thing to turn into a beauty contest." Sam recited the rules.

"My Dad called this, "the all cocks are created equal rule." Most men thought this rule related to cock size, but it had to do with playing with relations. My Uncle John thought he had the right to screw each of his nephews." Virgil broke in and gave more explanation.

"He didn't?" Bobby asked.

"Not at all. Uncle John thought he was too old to take a cock himself," Virgil replied. "To tell you the truth, after I spent some quality time tenderizing his prostate, he turned into a first rate bottom."

"Rule three is man sex is good and takes place in the open. Grand Dad was afraid guys would pair off and become lovers and there would be jealousy," Virgil explained. "Sex is public and group. The idea was to share the fun and the joy."

"The fourth rule is everyone has the right to say no. Sex is pleasurable and voluntary. Never do what you don't want done to you."

"Rule five is my favorite," Sam interjected. "No wasted cum!"

"How in hell do you waste cum?" I asked.

"Well, it's part of the biblical basis for the club. The first Virgil discovered man-to-man sex was fine, but he got worried about Onan. Onan sinned by spilling his seed on the ground. The traditional Christian interpretation was this dealt with masturbation. Virgil decided it was wasting sperm. If someone takes it and enjoys it, it isn't wasted."

"Deep in his heart he was a cum hound!" Bill cried. "It does have one nice side effect. Grange meetings are neat. No sticky goo on the floor." Bobby laughed.

"Do you need to suck it straight from the spigot or can you lick it up?" Bobby asked. Bobby lost his chance to play a virgin with that comment.

"Anyway you like it is fine!" Virgil said. Throughout the conversation, Virgil kept a close watch on Bobby's cock.

I always thought of Bobby as being young, but he knew just what to do. His cock firmed up from its relaxed state. He didn't get hard, just firmer. As he did, his wide slit opened a bit and a bead of precum oozed out. Virgil licked his lips; Bobby smiled at him.

"The rule applies to pre cum too," Virgil added, he moved across the tub and licked the precum from Bobby's cock.

I got out of the water and sat on the edge of the tub. I'm afraid I was already a bit above half-staff, but that didn't seem to bother my tub-mates at all. Sam slid across the tub like an otter and deep throated my cock in a single movement. He was no amateur at cock sucking. The afternoon was off to a good start

Chapter 2

Once Bobby and Virgil went at it, the atmosphere in the tub became intensely sexual. I could tell from the second his mouth touched Bobby's cock, Virgil's interest in man sex wasn't perfunctory. Sam was a dirty blond otter. He was deeply tanned and had a runner's body. Like Virgil, he had a long white snake hanging from between his legs. It was thin, with a big, purple, mushroom head. While Sam sucked on my cock, Bill got up and went over to Sam.

Bill was a surprise. He was a big, solid man, moderately hairy, but unlike many big men, his cock was perfectly in scale with his huge body. It was long, very thick and meaty. He was uncut, but he was excited enough for his cock head to part the puckered skin and peak out of the hood. I was sure when it reached full size it would be 10 inches. It was strange to think I had known him for years and it never occurred to me he was packing all that meat. I don't think of myself as a size queen, but I admit to feeling a definite attraction to his horse cock.

Sam stared at it like a deer in headlights. He had an opportunity to demonstrate his attraction to it and that he did. Sam began licking Bill's cock head as it emerged from the foreskin.

"We'll cook in this tub if we stay in here too long, let's adjourn to a bedroom," Virgil suggested, as he looked up from Bobby's cock. That was all right with everyone, so we got out, dried off and went to his bedroom. It was next to the tub area. Sam's room was an aging hippie's dream. Beautifully framed Grateful Dead posters and Warhol prints adorned the room, there was a water bed in the middle and beaded curtains on the door. The room was frozen in time. We got on the bed and relaxed.

"If you can, save your sperm for tomorrow," Virgil suggested. "I guess you don't need to worry about that, Bobby. I used to shoot four and five times a day, but us older guys need to save our resources." Virgil started sucking Bobby again. Bobby was always polite and he rotated so he could 69.

Bill came over to me. It's difficult to change a professional relationship to a sexual one. "Do you mind if I try out your cock?" Bill asked.

"If I get a lick or two of yours," I said. "I had no idea you were packing all that meat."

"You don't mind an uncut cock? Some guys seem to object," Bill replied.

"You are hanging out with the wrong crowd! No problem here at all," I replied. Much to my relief, Bill and I were sexually compatible. I never thought of myself as a size queen, but Bill's cock did exert some sort of a spell on me. He was a drooler and a twitcher. After a minute or two of my sucking on his monster, the sweet fluid began to flow and I knew all was well.

Bill and I seemed to think alike. It was clear we had similar sexual tastes and preferences. Sam joined in. Since Bill and I were in the 69 position he got on the bed and began nursing Bill's balls while I addressed the monster cock.

After a few more minutes, Virgil got up. "Guys, I seem to be at the point of no return here and need to stop. The men at the Grange like big loads. That's not a rule; it's just a preference. The more cum you shoot tomorrow the better it will be."

"I sure as hell don't want to stop," Sam added, "but I'm sure real close too. I would like to put on a good show tomorrow."

"Is there a contest for the most cum?" Bobby asked. Virgil laughed.

"Not really. But maybe we can get one organized," Virgil replied. "Some guys have the meat, some have the potatoes and others have the cream sauce. Years ago, Daddy said they had a member of the Grange named Billy Pounder. He had one big mother fucker and was damn proud of it. He was a suckee and didn't reciprocate. Well eventually, he got too embarrassed, so he had to suck someone. He picked Johnny Olsen, the guy with the smallest cock in the group."

"Well, Johnny was one of those who provided the sauce and poor Billy almost choked. Daddy said, he never figured out where Johnny kept all the sperm, but Billy made up for years of not cock sucking in that one orgasm by drinking the whole load. That's another one of the rules, once you start on a load, you have to take the whole thing. Billy swallowed and swallowed, but Johnny kept on ejaculating."

"Poetic justice?" Bill asked.

"More than you know," Virgil answered. "Billy figured he get even by fucking the shit out of Johnny. It turned out, Johnny was a fuck pig. He could take a School Bus up his ass and still want more. It was the best fuck of their lives. Johnny and Billy became lovers."

"I hate to sound like an old hippie, but the Grange is about as evenhanded a group of men as you would ever meet," Sam said. "Everything is in the open; sucking, fucking, shooting. We do everything for maximum pleasure. It's funny, I was a wild a crazy guy in San Francisco in my youth, but never approached what these guys do."

"You should have fit in from the start," I said.

"It was harder than you might think," Sam replied. "I had a difficult time admitting I liked cock. I was really active with women, but sneaked around for man sex. I guess you could say I was a macho asshole when I wasn't sucking cock."

"That sounds like the kind of thing that can cause problems," Bill said. "It was hard for me to get used to the possibility I was gay. I almost had a mental breakdown before I came to my senses."

"I almost became an alcoholic," Sam said. "My wife left me, but then I met Virgil. Virgil taught me how to be macho and a cock sucker."

"You sound like a great humanitarian!" I said to Virgil. He smiled.

The next day, we had a late breakfast and went wandering around Rapture. If you were to pick the most unlikely place in the world to be a center for homosexual sex, Rapture would be it. It was as ordinary as can be.

Around noon, Sam took us to the Lodge Hall. It was an undistinguished wood frame building on a back street of the town. I realized this had once been the main street, but modern traffic patterns had focused on other streets. There were a few other businesses on the street, other than an auto repair shop and a Seed and Feed store. The Grange was a bit run down, but not in real disrepair. The interior was just as undistinguished. Whatever the strengths of the Grange, interior decoration wasn't one of them. The entire place was painted eye saver green and was illuminated by 40 year old florescent fixtures.

Several men entered the building with us. They went to the doors on the right. We went to the doors on the left. We stripped naked and put our clothes in school type lockers.

"Is there an initiation?" Bobby asked. I had wanted to ask the same question. I didn't know if there was a club's ritualistic ceremony, or purely a social event.

"Not officially," Sam said. "I was greeted by the oldest and the youngest members. They were the reception committee and introduced me to the rest of the members. There wasn't a reception line, but I did get to meet most of the men."

"At my first meeting here, everyone wanted to have some genital contact. They officially claim it's a social club, but it sure as hell seemed to like cock. It's purely a sex club to me. One or two guys just fondled it. Most licked or sucked me before the end of the evening," Sam continued.

"No ass play?" I asked.

"Not unless you initiate it," Sam explained. "There are a lot of pats on the buns, but nothing will happen unless your hole is in play."

"If a finger wanders toward your ass, you either clamp shut or open wide depending on your mood?" Bobby asked.

"You got it," Sam said with a laugh. "I guess that applies to you, as well as to all of them. If you see a man's ass hole, he's telling you something. It's never by accident. A finger in your hole is a nice way to ask."

"Is that an official rule?" I asked.

"You're a scientist, that bit of information is purely derived from field observation," Sam said. "It works the other way around too. Just touch a hole and see if there is room for you at the inn."

"No hard feelings if you don't want to play?" I asked.

"None at all, as I said a very open group," Sam concluded. "Some of the men like younger guys. You may be really popular, Bobby. This may be a bit shocking to a kid your age."

"Thanks for the concern, Sam," Bobby said. "To tell you the truth, I'm excited by the prospects. I had some experience in rural Virginia and I liked what I did then. Most of the guys there were quite a bit older than me." We hadn't told him of our experiences at Hillbilly Hollow and I knew Bobby could handle himself as well as anyone. He had a typical young man's tolerance for sex. I smiled to myself. I had that same tolerance.

Virgil came to the door with two other men. As Sam had said, one was older and the other a lot younger. The older man looked a bit like Santa Claus and was introduced as Robert. His white beard seemed to merge with his chest hair. He had a belly and it was hard to see his cock. The young guy was Eddy. He was maybe 20, with a military style haircut and a tanned, smooth muscular body. His head was all but shaved, so the only hair on his body was a thick pubic bush. He was at half-staff already.

Eddy's eyes lit up when he saw me. I know puppy love when I see it and I also know when I run into someone who had a crush on Grizzly Adams when he was a kid. Eddy and I would get along fine. Robert was talking to Bobby and I could read him like a book too. Bobby was attractive and young and the older man was a classic old geezer. Robert was hoping against hope, hairy portly men didn't turn off the young man.

Sam and Virgil went off for a few minutes to discuss something leaving us alone for a few minutes. We made small talk. Eddy looked down and realized his erection was well beyond half-staff now. He blushed red. "I'm sorry," he said. I stroked it.

"You got some nice equipment there," I said. A glob of precum oozed out. With my finger, I spread it over his cock head, giving it a shine.

"You like it? You don't mind?" he asked with a surprised tone in his voice. I licked my finger, tasting his precum.

"Sure, that's the nice thing about naked men, you always know where you stand," I said. By this time, I was well beyond half-staff. Eddy looked at my cock and smiled.

"I see your point," he said as he reached out and stroked my cock. I looked over at Bob and Robert. Bobby was playing with Robert's tits and fluffing the thick hair on the older man's chest. As I watched, Robert cupped Bobby's low hangers in his hand. Bobby smiled and Robert dropped to his knees and took the boy's cock into his mouth. They both looked happy. Eddy took the same opportunity to service me.

I was ready and Eddy was an enthusiastic, but inexperienced sucker. Bobby and I were looking at each other while the two men sucked us. Eddy's held my balls to stabilize himself as he sucked. His index finger wandered back toward my ass hole. I adjusted my stance to give him easier access. Bobby smiled at me as he saw me accommodate Eddy.

Sam and Virgil returned.

"Don't wear them out before they meet the entire group!" Virgil said. Robert and Eddy got up. "Follow us." We went to a small door and then went down a narrow stair. The basement room was nice. It was a bit like an upscale health club. There was a glassed in shower to the side of the room. The floor was tiled up to a pillow covered benches on the edge of the room. There were beds perpendicular to the bench. There were several slings hanging from the ceiling. A table to one side had refreshments, soft drinks, beer and wine. There were perhaps 16-20 men in the room, all nude and varied in age and condition.

Most of the men were middle-aged with a few older and a few younger. Eddy introduced me to the men near the entrance.

"It looks like Eddy has explained the rules to you already," a soft spoken man named Jim said as he observed our erections. He was a slim, tall otter, covered in dark hair from his bushy beard to his toes. He was well tanned and obviously spent a lot of time outside. There was no tan line. His cock was still soft and almost lost in the tangle of his dense pubic bush.

"It looks like Eddy has made you feel welcome," a shorter man next to Jim said. He was Steve and was middle-aged, but in good condition. Jim dropped down to his knees and sucked Eddy. After saying hello Steve told me, he would be in one of the slings later and to feel free to take a poke.

"You are a total bottom?" I asked. A short, rather handsome bald bear with pure white beard came over to me, bent over and sucked my cock as I was talking to Steve.

"I use to be a pure top, but I tried the other side a few months ago. I didn't think much of it, but it's strange. I found myself thinking about it more and more," Steve said. "My best friend in this group, Earl, couldn't be here today. He's the usual occupant of one of the slings. He asked me, if I would take his place."

"It seems to me there's a long distance between trying out the bottom position and hitching yourself into a swing for a gang fuck," I said. "Are you ready?" Steve laughed.

"By the way, the polar bear sucking your cock is Byron," Steve said. "I guess it is a bit of a stretch, but we're all old friends here. I spent enough time over the years probing their insides with my cock. Earl gets really excited when he takes a half dozen cocks; he recommends it highly."

"Damn you've got a pretty one," Byron said as he got up from sucking me. "I'm Byron, as Steve said."

"I'm Gus. You do a good job on a cock."

"If you're after a virgin, you're going to need to look elsewhere," Byron replied. He looked around the room. "As a matter of fact, everyone in this room is experienced." Steve was on his knees now, replacing Byron on my cock. I reached over and put my hand on Eddy's buns. He didn't object at all. I slipped my hand towards the crack. Eddy looked at me and smiled.

Two almost identical men came over to us.

"Gus, these are the Peterson boys, Karl and Gustav," Eddy said. Both men were blond, beefy and solid looking. They were well above six feet tall and I guessed they were near 300 pounds.

"You look like twins," I said.

"We both took after Dad. I'm Karl and I'm three years older than Gustav here. Daddy always said when you get something right, don't mess with it."

"Although, even Dad had to admit, when our sister was born, she took after Mom," Gustav added. "There can be too much of a good thing."

"Wrestlers? Football players?" I asked.

"You got it. In High School we were in every sport that needed brawn and no brains," Karl said. "We run a small construction company now, Peterson Brothers. We got no imagination either." I laughed.

"The boys are the best builders in town," Jim said as he got up from his long session nursing Eddy's cock. At first, I thought the Peterson Brothers were smooth, but they were covered in fine, blond hair, which all but disappeared against their white skin.

"Let's go over to the bench where we can spread out," Karl suggested. He wanted to suck me, while I sucked his brother. In the course of the next hour, I made contact will all of the men at the party. The sex was affable and pleasant, rather than exciting.

We had been at play with the members of Rapture Grange for a good two hours when a new member of the Grange arrived late. I had been told the doors were locked after an hour, so I was a bit surprised.

The new arrival was a tall, tin, pale young, young man, with a boyish face. He was 30 to 35, but with a quick glance you might easily mistake him for 20. He caused a bit of a stir and several of the men were clearly excited by his presence.

When he stripped, the reason for the excitement became clear. If the man weighed 180 pounds, a good 90 of those pounds was hanging between his legs. Even soft, his cock was huge.

The soft member was 8" long, and a good 2" in diameter. Well-hung men would have been proud to have his soft cock; it was bigger than mine at full erection.

He walked directly over to me and introduced himself.

"Hi, I'm Peter Pounder. Sam called me and said we had some company," he said. He shook hands, but with his other hand, he fondled my cock. I was half-hard, so he coaxed some pre cum out. I returned the favor. His horse cock immediately responded.

"Damn, you're fucking handsome. I've always liked the Grizzly Adams type," he said. "Sam told me I'd like what I'd see here and damn if he isn't right."

"I like what I'm seeing too," I said. Peter took a drop of my precum on his finger and licked it. I stroked his cock a second time and it twitched. It grew a bit larger. "I especially like what I'm feeling," I added.

Peter leaned forward and whispered. "That's 100% pure cock drool I just licked, you're already revved up?" he said. "I'm getting a late start, but with one or two more strokes and I'll catch up with you." He looked me eye to eye."I was kind of hoping you were into big meat. Is there any chance you are a bottom?" I didn't need to answer. Peter knew what I wanted from the look in my eyes. We understood each other.

Chapter 3

Peter was popular with the men. I later found out he was the son of the Billy Pounder Virgil told me about earlier. Billy had a sense of humor, his son's name and hobby were the same. Peter was a pure top and could only get off with his monster buried deep in an ass. There were only a few who could take it in the Grange. He always made it a point to attend when there were new men who could potentially accommodate it.

I wasn't 100% sure I could take it, but I hadn't had trouble with other big cocks in the past and I sure was inspired. So was Peter. He got hard and the entire organ was spectacular. He had a normal size head, but the shaft bloated to almost three inches right behind it. It was wider than deep, but the sperm tube was clearly defined on the bottom side, as were the veins and arteries that fed blood to the monster.

The shaft tapered as it reached his body. I had seen this a few times before. The taper made a natural cock ring which trapped the blood in the dick and kept him hard. I had been fucked by a man with a smaller version of Peter's cock years before. He was hard for a good hour. I wondered if Peter could do the same.

"Let's go over to the sling. It makes it easier," Peter said. "I can get the prefect angle that way."

"For you or for me?"

"Both, I hope," he replied. "That's the way it's supposed to be, isn't it?" I said, yes. "Has anyone been up your ass today?"

"Nope, you are the first."

"I'd go slowly then. It's usually easier if you've been already fucked," Peter explained. "It opens you up some and gets some lube deep in your ass." He was serious about this; it seemed he was planning his approach carefully.

"I see you've made a study of this!" I said. "I'm no virgin. I never taken one as big as yours, but I sure am willing," Peter smiled. We were at the sling. I had never been in one before, but Peter knew the ropes, as it were.

"This usually attracts an audience," Peter whispered to me and he slipped my legs into the straps. "It's okay for guys to watch here. Did they tell you that?"

"Yes, no problem for me. I'm a little bit of an exhibitionist," I said. "Do you mind?"

"Nope, I seem to get an audience anyway." Peter said. "If anyone has a cock magnet, it's me. Guys almost trip over themselves trying to see it." As he spoke, he covered his cock in lube and began stroking himself hard. It didn't take too much effort to do that; he was excited. Peter was right about the magnetic qualities of his cock. As he got harder, the men seemed to congregate around us. Virgil, Eddy and the Peterson brothers were in the group, as well as three of four guys whose names I didn't recall.

"Would you like an ice breaker?" Virgil asked. "Eddy here would be glad to work some lube in your ass." I looked up at Peter.

"That would be a good idea, I think," Peter said. Eddy was next to him and lubricated his cock. He had a nice six or seven incher with a big, flared head. It popped in my ass effortlessly. It might have been a utility fuck to lubricate my ass tunnel, but Eddy was into it big time. He pulled out and added more lubricant and then re entered.

"Shoot some of your homemade, special sauce up there," Virgil ordered. "I don't think Gus would mind some cum-lube." Eddy must have been really close to shooting. He shot off almost immediately. After he completely unloaded, he pulled out.

"If it's deep you want, let me help you." A tall, thin, gawky guy spoke. I remembered him as Slim, a local farmer. He had a rock hard, but thin, 8 inch cock.

"Do you mind?" Virgil asked.

"No, if Peter doesn't mind sloppy seconds," I said. "There will be a lot of cum in there."

Peter laughed."No problem with me," he said. "I'm not the neatest guy in the world there's no way ass-sex can be perfect. The easier I slide, the better it is. Too tell you the truth; it seems to me the messier it is the easier it is." Slim had lubricated his cock and was ready.

"I know it ain't much to look at, Mister, but I'm a real good fucker," Slim said, as he poked his cock at my hole. "You'll like it." With that comment, he rammed me. His thin prong slipped in, through Eddy's cum and lodged deep in my rectum. I have to admit, I didn't have high expectations for Slim, but he turned out to be a first rate top. It took him three or four minutes to shoot and I enjoyed every minute of it. He began to shake and then added his seed to the mess of cum in my ass.

The audience had grown. Karl Peterson was playing with one of my nipples and an older man was stoking my cock. He squirted some lubricant on my dick. I had been hard for a while and the cool liquid felt great.

"You're a great looking guy," the older man said. "I'm Bert, the local pharmacist. I've had enough anatomy classes to give you a nice boost." He slipped his hand down from my cock and worked two fingers into my ass. They went right for my prostate and pressed it. A shiver of excitement raced through my body. "You've got a beautiful ass too. Peter, this boy's ripe and ready for picking."

As soon as he was done, Peter adjusted the sling to get my ass in the perfect position and he placed his cock nudging at my hole. He stopped before shoving it in.

He pushed the sling so it rocked slightly. "Are you ready?" Peter asked. I nodded. His cock head was normal sized so it popped through the sphincter easily.

"That's a good start!" Karl said. "I barely got that far."

Virgil was at my head and had a small net covered, glass ampoule.

"Burt gave me this to make the trip easier," Virgil whispered in my ear. He broke the ampoule and held it to my nose. I took a deep breath. It was pure amyl nitrate. I felt an explosion of desire, then a sharp pain. The pain lasted nor more than a second. I knew I was skewered. Peter had deep dicked me.

"Fucking beautiful!" Gustav cried. That's the way it felt to me too. Peter's huge member totally occupied me. My head was swimming; I couldn't think clearly, other than I desperately wanted to get it as deep as possible. Peter was still, but I undulated my ass to see if there was any way to intensify the feeling. Peter pulled out an inch or two, then thrust deep again. Virgil and the Petersons began to rock the sling.

Peter's cock head and the tapered base of his cock were perfect fits for my sphincter; the massive shaft was as big as I could possibly take. As I loosened up and relaxed, they rocked the sling and my ass began to accommodate itself to the invader. The first rocking motions were only one or two inches, but they grew. Virgil and the Petersons were controlling the motion of the sling. Eventually they increased the swinging motion to four to five inches and finally to the point where Peter's cock was free of my ass. I felt hollow for a second before the sling slipped forward and Peter's cock was fully lodged in my rectum.

The feelings were incredibly intense and odd. In some ways, it was pure cock pleasure. Because of the sling, the only contact between Peter and me was his cock and my ass. The audience was very appreciative.

"Slim, is that your cum or Eddy's that's squishing out beside Pete's cock?" Robert asked.

"I don't rightly know," Slim answered in his country drawl. "Why don't you get some and give it the old taste test. If anyone knows what my sperm tastes like it's you." Everyone laughed.

"Can you rest a minute Peter and let me try it?" Robert asked.

"Sure but only a minute!" Peter replied. Peter pulled out. I felt hollow. A split second later, I felt a tongue at my ass. Robert was licking up the juice that had oozed from my hole. He licked for maybe 30 seconds, moved out of the way and Peter was back.

"It must be Eddy's, yours must be in too deep," Robert said. I was getting tired, Virgil must have noticed.

"We need a rest break here, the shows over for a while," he said. Peter pulled out again and the Petersons helped me out of the sling.

"Damn Gus, I like you more and more!" Karl said. "I've never seen anyone take Peter that easily. It was beautiful." Peter came up to me.

"Are you okay?" he asked with genuine concern in his voice.

"It was good, real good," I answered. "It is a challenge, though, but worth the effort."

"It was great for me. I've never met anyone who could take it so easily," Peter whispered. "Do you think we could do it again? It's okay if you say no; I understand."

"I'm ready when you are," I said. "Would you mind if I sat on it?"

"Shit no. I love it that way," he said as we went over to one of the benches on the side of the room. "Do you want to shoot while I'm fucking you?" he asked.

"I kind of had my heart set on it." I said.

"Let me sit down, than you sit back on it. I'll hold you steady," he said. "You know there's a rule, no spilled cum. That position makes it easy for someone to suck you when you pop." There were several guys with us. I guessed there would be no problem finding a volunteer.

Peter sat down; I sat back on his cock. By now, it slipped deep with only a slight twinge of pain when the thickest part of his organ entered. He held me tight.

"Hitch up your legs on top on mine." Peter told me. I did and for a brief second my entire weight was on his cock. I hooked my legs on top of his. He began to spread his legs wide. This stretched my asshole wide too, making it impossible for me to resist anything he tried to so with his cock. For the audience this was a great position. They could see my rock hard cock and balls, his low hangers and as much of his cock as wasn't in my ass.

The Peterson men got involved. Karl bent over to suck my cock. Gustav took care of Peter and my balls. With a monster cock in my ass, Karl sucking my cock and Gustav at my balls, things were good. They got better.

Gustav was the quiet one of the brothers and had seemed a bit shy. He would lick my balls, and then transfer his attention to Peter's low hanging ball sack. He surprised me when he licked Peter's cock on the out strokes and then tried to get his tongue into my hole with the monster cock. I was being rimmed while being fucked. Vigil popped another ampule of amyl and gave both Peter and me a good snort. We both went in for the kill. He was frantically trying to ram me deeper and I was wiggling my ass to force my prostate into closer contact with his meat.

Peter began to cry out as he shot his load into the deepest recesses of my ass. I began to shoot and my ass contracted, so I felt as if my ass was a milking machine, squeezing the man seed out of his bloated cock.

Karl was there to take my load. My cock head becomes unbelievably sensitive during an orgasm, and I always pull it away from a sucker as I shoot. It is so sensitive it almost hurts. Karl must have realized this and he showed me no mercy at all. He was like a starved baby at his mother's breast. I almost passed out. I don't exactly know what was going on around me, but I think I heard applause. We sat there still. Karl continued to suck me and induce additional ejaculations until he completely drained my balls.

As Peter relaxed, his cock contracted until it was a normal cock again. It eventually plopped out of my ass. Gustav was there, he took Peter's cock drool, then rimmed me again, cleaning up my asshole with his tongue. I got up and almost fell on the floor. The whole thing had taken more out of me than I had realized.

"Just relax and get on your hands and knees," Karl said. "You've got a beautiful ass, Gustav loves it. Let him munch on it for a while, please. He'd love it." I didn't know why, but I did as he asked. Gustav was back at my ass for the next twenty minutes. It was very relaxing. I was getting a bit stiff, when Virgil came up and told Gustav to take a break.

I got up on a bench and lay down. Virgil's cock was at eye level. I was going to suck it, but his cock was covered in lube and rock hard. It turned out he wanted to fuck. His cock slipped into my ass easily. It was hard to believe I was being fucked again. It was even harder to believe I was enjoying it as much as I was. Slim came up to us and whispered in Virgil's ear.

"Do you want to try something special?" Virgil asked. I nodded. He pulled out and Slim slipped in again. Then Virgil and Slim got on the floor and intertwined, with their cocks together.

"Try to sit on them." Slim asked. "The two aren't any thicker than Peter's." I straddled the pair of cocks and sat down. After a couple of false starts, they both got in and I slid down the pair, trapping both in my ass. It was okay for me, but great for Virgil and Slim. They had the stimulation of my ass and the other guy's cock rubbing against their member. Virgil shot off first. He was a bucker and it was a wild ride.

Virgil's cock shrank after the orgasm and fell out of my ass. Slim stayed in, but pulled out without shooting. "The day is still young," he said. It had been quite an experience, but I decided to get up and roam around before someone else got in my ass. I was real near my quota, for a while at least.

"You put on a good show!" a man said. "Jacob Martin here, they call me JM. I've never seen anyone take Peter so easily. It was a joy to watch."

"I didn't expect to be so much on display," I said. Martin was short, thick man with thinning dirty blond hair and a hairy chest. He was middle aged and I could tell he had been quite muscular when he was younger.

"You've got nothing to be ashamed about in the show department," JW said. "You're new here. We all like a show and it's no problem. It's really nice to have a guy get into it as fast as you did. You brought out the best in Eddy. He's never fucked in the open before. It looked to me as if he liked it. I've been hoping to get his cock up my ass ever since he joined. There may be a chance now." He got close to me and played with the hair on my chest. "You are the hairy one, aren't you?" I reached down and cupped is balls and cock in my hand. He had a nice set. He was also completely relaxed.

JM's mouth was at my tit level so he licked it. Much to my surprise after the massive fuck fest I had been in for the last half hour, I was hard as a rock.

"I need a cock in my ass to get hard," JM said.

"Is that an invitation?" I asked.

"Sure as shit it is!" he said. We were next to a bench so he got down and hoisted his legs on my shoulders. "Don't worry about lube, I took care of that earlier," he said, "and you don't need to worry about being too polite. I don't mind it a bit rough. Guys tell me I'm really tight, but don't worry. I like it."

He wasn't kidding about being tight. Fortunately, he wasn't kidding about the liking it part either. Usually, once you get in the ass, it becomes easy going. JM has buns of steel. It was as if he wanted to trap my cock in his ass and keep it there. It was also clear some pain was involved, but his cock was hard and leaking the whole time. He was enjoying it. Eddy came up to us.

"I see you met my old boss, JM?" he said. He straddled JM's head and dangled his cock in his former boss' mouth. With one or two licks, Eddy got hard, so he shifted a little and let JM lick his balls.

"He has one tight ass!" I said. "It's quite an experience. Have you ever tried him out?"

"Nope, can't say that I have." Eddy said.

"It sure looks like you are ready," I said. "Why don't you come here and give him a poke?" JM twitched in excitement as the prospect of getting Eddy's cock in his ass became almost real. Eddy didn't say anything, but he pulled his balls from JW.'s mouth and stood next to me.

"He's really tight?" Eddy asked.

"He sure is. I'll bet the cock head of yours will stretch him wide open," I replied. I pulled out and Eddy took my place. It did take some doing to get Eddy's big mushroom in JW's hole, but it was worth it for both of them. After about ten minutes of fucking, I left them and moved on. There was no way JM would let Eddy out of his ass. I don't think Eddy had any intention of leaving his ass without a full deposit.

Chapter 4

I was wandering around trying to decide what to do next when Virgil rang a bell. "Break time!" he yelled. "If you can't shoot off in a minute, calm down and save it for later. Shower off and let's rest a little and get refreshed."

I went to the shower area and cleaned up. When I got out, they had brought in trays of sandwiches, fruit and deserts. The food was good, light, but satisfying.

Bobby came over to me and we traded notes. "It's wild here. You and Peter put on quite a show," he said. "It's sort of like a polite, upscale Hillbilly Hollow."

"The Hollow was on the fringe of society. These guys are 100% middle Americans," I said. "I assume you have been busy?"

"Robert's a nice guy. I've been making him and his friends really happy," he replied. "It's lucky a cock can't get calloused from being sucked too much." Virgil came over to us.

"I forgot to tell you about the break. It use to be most of the men had to get back to the farm to milk the cows. Now the break gives the married men a chance to get home for dinner," Virgil explained. "Originally this was the end of the meeting, but now we have a second session. It's for the men who work on Saturdays, or have other things to do during the day. You don't need to stay if you don't want too." He leaned closer to us. "The second session isn't quite as genteel. Construction workers, auto mechanics and guys like that make up the majority of the late comers," he whispered. "Most of them are bachelors and they really get into it." Virgil winked at us.

"Are you game?" I asked Bobby.

"Sure. I don't mind some variety at all." Frankly, I didn't need to ask. Bobby and I are a lot alike. Eddy came over to us and talked for a while.

"Are you enjoying yourselves?" he asked.

"It's a nice group of men," I said. "Friendly is hardly the word for them."

"That's one way to say it," Eddy said. "I've really enjoyed it this time. Things seem to be clicking."

"You look relaxed," I said. "Are you feeling comfortable with the group?"

"I guess I must be. I'm local here, but no one in my family has ever been a part of this, so it's all new to me. It takes some getting use to," he said.

"How did you find out about it?" Bobby asked.

"My best friend in High School told me about it. We had been messing around since grade school. I guess you could say he was more realistic than I was. He knew it was sex and he liked it a lot. I thought of it as messing around and pretended I didn't like it that much. Don got pissed at me and told me either I could admit I liked it, or we would stop," Eddy explained.

"We went for a month or two without playing and I finally gave in. Somehow, when we started messing around again, the sex was twice as good. He told me about the Grange and asked if I wanted to try it out," he continued. "We went visit Sam to talk about it and Virgil dropped in. We got into it pretty heavy. I was a little scared and embarrassed, but the sex was so good I had to join. Actually, I didn't think I wanted to, but I couldn't bear the thought of missing the sex. I guess that means I really wanted to all along. I've been to three meetings and this is the best."

"You know all these men?" Bobby asked.

"I know most. At first, it was kind of hard to be naked with the men I've known for years," Eddy said. "I never expected to see them here at all. They don't seem to be the type."

"I'm I the type you'd expect to see here?" I asked.

Eddy looked at me a smiled. "Not in a million years," he said. "I'm afraid I've got too many strange ideas of what a gay guy is supposed to look and act like. I sure am glad you are here." JW came up to us and joined the conversation.

"Damn, this has been a good day. Gus, I think you're the reason," he said.

"Thanks, but I think Eddy played a role in that," I said.

"It was really good JW; I enjoyed it a lot," Eddy said.

"Not half as good as it was for me," J.W. replied. "You know, I was a confirmed top for years. I had the stupid idea it was more macho to fuck than to be fucked. When I finally took a cock in my ass, I couldn't believe how good it was. My magic nut almost exploded when you rammed me, Eddy. I'm not sure about the anatomy, but when your cock head squeezed my prostate, I will swear some sex hormones squirted into my blood. It was good to watch you enjoy yourself so much, Eddy."

"Was it that obvious?" Eddy asked.

"Eddy, it's pretty obvious every man here likes it and likes it a lot," Bobby said. "Men can't hide a whole lot when they're naked. Are you staying for the second session?"

"I usually don't, but I think I will, this time," Eddy said. "Somehow, I had twice as much sex as usual and I still want more."

I was feeling relaxed and refreshed. I had been tired, but the food and the shower left me feeling great and ready to go again. The crowd had thinned out quite a bit. I noticed one or two faces I didn't know. Robert came up to me and introduced several new Grange members.

"Gus, Bobby, this is Mitch and Lou, they run the Rapture Auto Repair. We shook hands. Lou was small, wiry, and muscular. Mitch was a dark, bear like man, with a very somber look on his face. We shook hands as another man came up to us.

"Hi, I'm Sean the local fag florist!" he announced. "You're new here aren't you?" Before I had a chance to say anything, he was on his knees sucking Bobby.

"Sean's kind of loony," Mitch said in an extraordinarily deep voice. "He's the reserved type." Sean and Lou laughed. I looked the new men over. Lou was ultra masculine in appearance but half sized. He was barely five feet tall. He was hairy and well groomed and obviously was careful about his appearance. His cock was cut and almost pretty.

Mitch would have looked like the missing link, but he tended toward the primate side of evolutionary development. He was shaggy and ungroomed. He pulled his hair back in a pony tail and didn't shave. The hair was continuous from just below the bald spot on the top of his head to his toes, except for his eyes, a pink tongue and the palms of his hands. The soft tip of his uncut cock peeked out from a thicket of hair in his crotch.

"Damn, you're handsome," Mitch said, looking at me. He looked shocked and embarrassed. I realized he was thinking aloud and the comment had just escaped.

"Thanks," I replied.

Mitch got close to me and whispered, "You like man sex?"

"That's why I'm here," I answered.

"Lou and I like it too. Do you want to play with us?" he asked. "You don't have to if you don't want to. We understand."

I reached into the thicket of hair at his crotch and played with his cock. Mitch made a motion with his hand and a second later Lou was at my cock, sucking.

"Are you and Lou a couple?" I asked.

"Pals," Mitch said, "real good pals." By now, I had a good grip on his cock. If you evaluated cocks by volume rather than length, Mitch was big. His cock rivaled Peter's in thickness, but was six inches long. It also had a pronounced upward curve.

"Nice beer can you have," I said. Mitch smiled. I reached behind his cock and found his balls. Most beer can cocks have a compact set of matching balls. Mitch had bull balls, hanging low and free in a hairy ball sack.

"If you like cream, I've got lots of it," Mitch said. "I've been saving up for a few days. Let's get off to the side where we can spread out some." The three of us shifted to a corner of the room. By now, there were a number of new men in the Grange Hall.

Mitch took over the sucking duties as soon as we relocated. He looked crude, but he was a delicate and careful sucker. He was one of those guys who seemed to worship the cock. I tend to think of a cock as a toy and plaything. For Mitch it was an object of worship and veneration. I got Lou's cock in my mouth and we all had an enjoyable interlude.

I wanted to get Mitch's beer can in my mouth, but Mitch resisted. "I like to suck," he said, "You don't need to." I told him I wanted to and eventually I insisted and he gave in. His cock was a trip. The hair grew halfway up the shaft. He had a lot of extra skin, so his cock was completely enshrouded in foreskin even when hard. I peeled the skin back, exposing his head. It was big, plump and the size of an apricot. It was purple-blue, cut in half by his wide piss slit. I pulled the slit open and worked my tongue into the opening.

He had been oozing pre cum for the entire time he sucked me. The foreskin trapped all this goo and it had ripened. It might be more accurate to say it had fermented. The smell and taste was strong and pungent. It also turned me on big time. I was taking the fresh precum oozing from his slit and mixing it with the aged brew, stored in his foreskin. It was a real treat.

While Mitch hadn't wanted me to suck him, once I did, he was more than appreciative. He reacted to every movement of my mouth and tongue on his genitals. Somewhere in his massive body, there must have been a sex amplifier. I sucked him for a good ten minutes. By the time I was done, he was jelly.

"We need to cool down," I said as I pulled away from his cock. "I need to catch my breath."

"Can we do it again later?" he asked. He had panic-stricken look in his eyes.

"I'm planning on it, let's shower off and get a drink," I said. The three of us went to the showers. I saw Bobby had Sean in a sling and was fucking him in front of a group of admirers. The Johnson brothers joined us at the refreshment table.

"You guys hitting it off?" Gustav asked.

"It sure feels that way to me." I said. "Are you old friends?"

"Sure, we went to school together with Lou. Mitch is what they call a new comer here, only been in Rapture for 20 years!" Someone came up and tapped Mitch on the shoulder. They wanted him on the other side of the room. He asked, if was okay for him to go. I said, sure and he and Lou left.

"What is their story?" I asked. "Lovers?"

"More like father and son," Karl said. "Mitch came here with his Dad. Dad was an ex-con and scared the town half to death; he beat on Mitch something awful. He was killed in the accident that killed Lou's folks. Strangely enough, it was Lou's folks who caused the accident. They ran a stop sign. Lou suffered severe brain damage in the accident. Mitch sort of adopted Lou and has been with him ever since." It just then struck me Lou hadn't said a word since we met.

"There are some really small minds in small towns. Some have never forgiven Mitch for having the father he did. He thinks he's an ugly bastard and has what they now call 'self esteem' problems. He's a great mechanic and it's hard to believe Lou is the person who got out of the hospital 15 years ago. I had him pegged as a vegetable for the rest of his life. He can walk and function as long a Mitch is near."

"He's so handsome and well groomed. I never would have guessed," I said.

"Believe it or not, that's Mitch's doing. Lou was a bit of a dandy in High School. He came out of the hospital looking like hell. Mitch fixed him up and that's when things began to get better for Lou. He could at least look in the mirror and see the person he once was," Karl continued. "They have a quiet life. The Grange is the only time they get to have some fun. That is Virgil's doing. He got them in. Virgil's a great cock sucker and a true Christian."

"Who's the new meat?" A voice boomed out. A short, scrawny man with a deep voice appeared next to Karl.

"Freddy, you have absolutely no sophistication at all! This is Gus, a visitor to the Grange," Karl said. "Gus, this is Freddy Mills, the plumber you hire if the good ones are too busy!" Freddy laughed.

"Looks to me like you have some extra pipe hanging between your legs," I said. Freddy wasn't a looker, but he was hung.

"It's usually a drain pipe, but sometimes I use it as a supply."

"Feeding tube?" I asked. Freddy thought that was about as funny as anything he had ever heard.

"If you're lucky," he replied. "Has anyone ever told you, you look like Grizzly Adams?"

"One or two," I said. Mitch and Lou returned from the conversation on the other side of the room.

"How goes things, Freddy?" Mitch asked. Freddy launched himself at Lou's cock and began sucking like a maniac. "Well, I guess things are the same as last time." Mitch said smiling. Lou was obviously pleased by the attention. Freddy was getting hard and that seemed to attract some glances. When he got up, he looked as if he might fall over he was so unbalanced. Peter walked over and a crowd gathered. Big cocks can be magnetic; certainly, they were in the Rapture Grange. There was a lot of discussion about whose cock was largest, but then Bill and another man came over. They were hung like Peter and Freddy.

I hadn't seen Bill except in a far corner for most of the day. He had been a private party with an old friend. The man with him, Red, owned a construction company. He was a big, solid man, with the whitest skin I had ever seen and copper colored hair. Red's cock was a solid tube of white flesh hanging from his copper bush. He was uncut, but his cock head made no mark on the foreskin.

Apparently, Bill, Freddy, Red and Peter hadn't been to the same meeting in a while and the Grange members seemed to look on it almost as a planetary conjunction. Four monster cocks in the same room impressed everyone: it was a good sign. There were murmurings of possibilities presented by the extra meat.

"Can you take one that big?" Mitch asked. I told him I had already taken Peter's earlier in the day. Mitch looked impressed. "How about Red?" Mitch asked. "Red's a nice guy; he's a friend of mine. I've never been able to take a cock that big, but it turns me on to watch."

"He looks like a nice guy," I said. Virgil was talking with the four men. They were listening intently and then burst out laughing. Red said, "That's a plan!" and slapped Virgil on his back. Virgil turned to the group.

"Listen up guys. I can't remember the last time the Big Four were here. It seems to me this is a special occasion and we should celebrate it somehow. There's been a lot of talk about who has the biggest. Well, there's the biggest soft cock and the biggest hard one, but we were thinking what really counts is the way it feels in your ass. Who gives the biggest bang for the buck, as it were," Virgil explained.

"Now, if some guys were to volunteer to get fucked by these fine gentlemen," Virgil continued, "they could evaluate each for length, thickness and effectiveness." The crowd hooted in approval. "Now this is all done in the interest of science you know. Are there some volunteers?" The group dissolved into small groups, trying to get someone who was willing to be quadruple fucked. As usual with monster meat, there were more lookers than takers.

"I'm sure willing to try," Sean, the florist said. "But I need a second to fill in for me in case I get split in half. I'm pretty sure I can do two or three, but I just don't know about four. What happens if I shoot off after two?"

"Sean, I thought you told me you took the entire crew of the USS Enterprise once!" Jim said.

"I did, but that was over two days and I was inspired by patriotic pride and fervor!" Sean answered. The room burst out in laughter.

"I'd be glad to be your second!" Bobby said. "After that session we had in the sling, I'm pretty sure you will take at least three without mussing your hair." I was watching the hung men and could swear Red's and Fred's cocks twitched at the prospect of fucking Bobby. Bobby noticed too.

"I don't mind giving it a try," I said. "I kind of like new experiences."

"Lou and I will give Gus some back up," Mitch said. He put his arm around me and I could sense his excitement.

"The two new guys have stepped up to the plate, as has Sean, we need two more. Let's show some of that old Grange spirit!" Virgil urged.

A tall, thick man stepped forward. He looked like a retired Marine. "I'll give it a try," he said. I've never done cocks that big before, but I sure am willing!" There was applause.

"Thank you Charles," Virgil said. "Do you have a back up?"

"Yes sir! Charles Jr. has offered to help," he said with pride. There was a younger version of Charles standing next to him.

"Are you ready for this, Junior?" Virgil asked.

"Hell, yes! I've already had some practice with Freddy and Red. I'm the one who talked Daddy into it!" The room burst out in laughter again.

"Any more volunteers?" There was silence.

"Well I guess I will step up to the plate," Virgil said. "Sam, will you be my back up?" Sam nodded.

"What position do we take?" Bill asked. "Doggy style? Spread Eagle?"

"It seems to me, spread Eagle is the way to go. It gives the deepest penetration," Virgil said. "It also gives the best view to the audience."

"I can't see from back here," someone cried.

"Well, get in the front row on your hands and knees." Virgil said. "Open your ass wide and see if anyone goes for the gold!" There was more laughter, but three came forward and assumed the position.

I was on the floor with Bill at my ass. Charles was to my left with Freddy positioned at his hole; Virgil to my right with Red in the position. To Virgil's right, Peter was preparing to plow Sean. Each group had a tube of lubricant and a bottle or two of poppers. Mitch was lubricating my ass while Lou lubed Bill's cock.

Charlie Junior was lubricating his father's ass and telling him how good Freddy's cock felt. Charles was really turned on. "If you shoot off, I'll eat it all up, Daddy," Junior said. "I've never tasted the seed that made me, but I'm ready for it." I had the sense that Junior was trying to get his father to shoot off as soon as possible so he could get fucked by the other men.

Bill's cock was at my hole. He was pushing, but not hard enough to get in unless I relaxed completely. "Are you ready?" Bill asked. As he asked, he pushed harder, not hard enough to force it in, but there was real pressure. It was strange to have a man I had known for years forcing his cock into my ass. We had been friends and colleagues and I was worried this might change things. I was tense.

"A little more lube," I said. Bill pulled out and coated his cock head again. He had a club cock, with his head the same size as his shaft. He was uncut, but was so hard you couldn't tell.

"Ready now?" he asked. He was pressing harder now. I relaxed a second and he was in; he was all the way in. His big cock filled me up physically and emotionally. Every nerve in my ass and cock immediately linked up with its opposite nerve in Bill's cock. I thought Bill's cock might not stop. It would slide into my ass, through my intestines and end up nuzzled against my heart. It stopped well short of that. I was almost disappointed.

I almost passed out it felt so good. When I came out of the sexual trance and looked at Bill, I saw he was feeling the same things. He slowly pulled out, stopping for time to time, thrusting quickly when he saw me react. After a minute or so, I began to hear what was going on around me.

Freddy and Charles were having a good time. It had been an easy penetration and all was well. Red was only half way in Virgil's love tunnel. Virgil was hard as a rock and was enjoying the slow ride. Sean was moaning and crying. He screamed, "You're going to rip me in half!" but that was soon followed by, "Shove it deeper, deeper into my boy pussy!"

Bill rammed me hard and I slipped back into a fuck induced coma.

"Shit! I'm cumming!" Sean screamed. There was scurrying around as someone jumped to catch his sperm. Bobby would have to take the next three cocks. A bell rang. The first session was over.

"We have to do this again tonight," I said to Bill.

"Damn right!" he replied. We all got up and stretched ourselves and then got back into position. The fuckers rotated to the left so Charles got Bill; I got Red; Peter got Virgil and Freddy got to fuck Bobby.

Red was a utilitarian fucker. He was a bit crude in technique, but fun. He was vigorous, but not imaginative. He would ram the exact same place twenty or thirty times. I thought it was boring at first, but I soon found out my prostate had a very different opinion on the subject. After his slow fuck of Virgil, he appreciated my willingness to be pounded.

Bill's cock was as much as Charles could take. He was moaning; Junior was encouraging him to open wider. Junior was also stroking his Dad's cock. I saw Charles' entire body twitch. Junior was on his Dad's cock in a split second, sucking up the sperm spewing from the cock.

As soon as Charles got out of the way, Junior was in his place and Bill was deep in the boy's ass. I think it was a bit more than he expected, but Junior was willing to be opened wider. The bell rang again. This time when I got up I could see the audience was getting into it. Several guys were taking it doggy style and most of the cocks were hard or dripping.

I saw Bobby and asked how he was doing. He said Freddy was a piece of cake. I told him Bill had really hit the spot with me. I was to take Peter again. I was surprised to find Virgil had dropped out. He had shot off as Peter pulled out of him. Sam would take Fred

The third rotation was more intense than the earlier ones. Bill was near Bobby's upper limit in size, but they both wanted it deep, so there was some heavy lifting. Sam hadn't been fucked all day, so his ass was tight and Fred's cock seemed to grow with each penetration. Junior had been fucked by Red before, but not the way Red did it this time.

Peter was just as big as he had been in the morning. My ass had relaxed after the two previous fuckings, so his cock went deeper. It was just as intense as in the morning, but very different, more relaxed. It was as if I was being fucked by another man.

The bell rang and we stopped for a final time. There was no break. The fuckers were revved up now and wanted to shoot. The fuckees were all open and ready. Freddy was at my ass. It was an easy and pleasant fuck. The shot his load when I tightened my ass ring.

Red was attracted to Bobby and the two of them did a fuck ballet. Red skewered Bobby, and then lifted him up and walked around the room. Red's massive cock supported Bobby. Red bounced Bobby as they walked and I could tell the massive cock was getting deeper into Bobby's rectum.

I had seen Bobby enjoy himself many times before, but this was different. Red shot off on one of the bounces, shooting his seed deeper in Bobby's ass than ever before.

Bill's cock was too big for Sam, but Sam liked it so much he must have made room. It was a joint effort at accommodation.

When Peter's cock slid into Junior's ass, the boy all but died and went to heaven. It was as good as it could be. Junior and Peter were a perfect fit. Strangely, nobody was watching me by the time Freddy fucked me. Everyone in the room was fucking or sucking. Freddy was good but near his limit. He shot off after two or three strokes. When Freddy popped and pulled out I saw Mitch standing back and motioned for him to come over. He was hard, so I pulled up my legs and opened my ass for him. His beer can cock must have been planned as a prostate ram. It hit mine head on every penetration. When it got too intense, I made him stop and let Lou fuck me some. He loved it.

Mitch was on the floor next to me when Lou pulled out of my ass, straddled me and then sat on my cock. When he was fully impaled, Lou shot off. Mitch leaned over and sucked the spewing cum directly from the cock.

Chapter 5

Things settled down rapidly after the round Robin fucking. It had been good for the fuckers, fuckees and the watchers. In fact, it was hard to tell who had enjoyed it the most. We got back to Sam's Bed & Breakfast at 10:00 or so and slept really well. I woke at 8:00 smelling bacon.

I went to wake Bobby but he wasn't in his bed. I heard some noises from Bill's room. The door was ajar so I looked in. Bobby was sitting on Bill's cock. He was doing a good imitation of the hula-hula dance. He would rise up and then lower himself on the massive pole. Bobby's slim body was quivering like a leaf and it was hard to believe the Jim's massive cock could fit in the boy's ass. I closed the door and went down to breakfast.

Fifteen minutes later, Bill and Bobby joined me. Sam had a traditional breakfast; there was no trace of the food police in his menu. It was bacon, eggs, butter and coffee; it really hit the spot.

Mitch stopped by and told us how much he had enjoyed the meeting the day before. "I've never seen Lou enjoy himself more. Your cock is the first to tickle his prostate. He's never done that before," Mitch said.

"He seemed to like it," I said. "I'm not sure I have the ideal starter cock, but given the horse hung men at the meeting, I guess I was a good size."

"It was good for Lou. He doesn't take the initiative often. He just does what I tell him to do. Lou got excited watching the fuck-a-thon. He was really excited. He copies what I do, but when he sat on your cock, that was all Lou. I didn't coach him at all," Mitch said. "Maybe something is coming back. Brain cells can grow, you know." Mitch was proud of Lou's achievement and almost on the edge of tears. "You will come back, won't you?"

"It's a long drive here, but I had a great time," I said. "I've got a bad schedule for the next few months, but if I can make it again, I will. How many times do you get fucked by horse cocks like I did last night?"

"Don't worry, Mitch," Bill said, "I came here just to experience it once. I've been back a good ten times. Sex is a basic human instinct. Nowhere is it as good and plentiful as it is at the Grange."

"Please do," Mitch said, "Lou would love it. Shit, I'd love it."

"We call all agree on that!" I said. We had to get back so we packed up after breakfast and were on the way by ten.

"Was it a successful trip?" Bill asked once we were in the car and on our way.

"What do you think?" I asked. "Do you like cocks as much as I do?"

"I think I do," Bill said. "I like men period. It's funny. You and I are about as well educated and sophisticated as men get, but when confronted by our sex drive, sex drive wins every time."

"Do you think that's bad?" Bobby asked. "It seems pretty good to me."

"You may be right," Bill answered. "We are brought up to think our natural instincts and desires are bad. To do what comes naturally is a sin. I don't think that's right."

"The mistake is to lump all natural instincts together. Men have destructive urges, but they have creative urges too," I said. "The sex drive surely is the original creative instinct. I think most sexual problems derive from suppressing sexual instincts, not from expressing them."

"Everyone at the Grange was sure laid back about sex, naked and ready to play. It was nice," Bobby said. "No one was picking a life partner; they were just using their bodies to give pleasure. How in hell can that be bad?"

"It sure builds up as you get into it," Bill said "The excitement grows the more men are involved."

"Where were you during the first part of the meeting, Bill?" I asked

"After all this talk about the joys of group sex, I'm a bit embarrassed," Bill said. "I was with an old friend, Rob. He's a judge and was too afraid of exposure, but he wanted the sex too much to stay away. He's a good man and I understood his concerns. By the way, he'd be interested in meeting you, the next time you visit the Grange."

"Nice guy?"

"Yes, hung and furry like a gorilla. Sort of Sean Connery like."

"That sure sounds good to me," I said.

We weren't able to get to the next meeting of the Grange, but Bill and I were able to get to the Thanksgiving meeting. It was the week before Thanksgiving and Bobby couldn't get away from exams at school. Bill brought along a friend, Tony, a graduate student and the friend's lover, Mike. Tony was Italian, about six feet-two inches with curly black hair and a bushy mustache. A doctoral student, he was about 35 and had taught several years in a small college.

He was a friend of Bill's and shared the same sexual interests, but they apparently weren't lovers. Tony was working on Dionysian Rituals as a forerunner for Greek drama as his dissertation. Bill told him the Grange was as close as he would get in the United States.

Mike was a bland, blond man of about 40 who looked as if he was 25. He was small and slight. He was the vice president of a small bank. He also seemed to be shy.

"To tell you the truth," Tony said, "when Bill told me about the Grange, it seemed too good to be true. The Grange might approach the sexual abandon of the Greek festivals. I was excited, but it took some talking to get Mike to come along."

"I just didn't know what it would be like," Mike said. "Tony said it was purely research, but quite frankly…"

Bill laughed. "The Grange meeting took some getting use to for me. Sex was always hidden and secret. Being with men who were nude, hard and frankly interested in sex was a shock. It was good, but not what I had expected."

"How do you mean?" Mike asked.

"Well, it's not a beauty contest and you aren't looking for a date," I said. "In some ways at the Grange, you make your body and genitals available for other men's pleasure. In return, they do the same. It's very even handed."

"It's not just everyday sexual pleasure. I think the Greeks discovered that you could amplify the fun through the group's enthusiasm and participation," Bill said. "I think for the Greeks it was a social safety valve. They lived in a restrictive society and ritual festivals gave you a chance to let off steam in a socially acceptable way. As far as I can tell, the private lives of the Grange members are good and stable with very few divorces. I think most men aren't naturally monogamous. Several times a year at the Grange, you get a chance to have all the sex you want. Afterward, you go home and have no need to wander or experiment."

"Is it all sucking?" Mike asked.

"Not by a long shot," I said. "It's anything that rings your chimes. Some men like sucking and cuddling, others are into heavy duty fucking. It depends on you. Remember, it's okay either to look or to participate."

"It's better to watch and participate!" Bill said. Mike still looked a bit unsure, but the drive was pleasant and he seemed to relax as he came to know us better. He was your traditional MBA type with rather limited general knowledge. We were talking about primitive tribes and rituals and he was interested. When we reached Rapture, Sam came out to greet us. Rather to my surprise, Mike and Sam hit it off. The minute Mike saw Sam's collection of old rock concert posters they were pals.

Sam had been to concerts of the Beatles and Rolling Stones that were all but mythical events to Mike. Sam had been naked at Woodstock and Sam's "be free, be beautiful" hippy's approach to sex made sense to Mike in a way that my Ancient Greek rituals did not.

It was so obvious Mike and Sam hit it off, I was afraid Tony would be disturbed. That wasn't a problem. Tony was deep into the Dionysian ritual potential of the Rapture event and was having a great time talking with Bill and me. He wasn't interested in ancient American Rock and Roll history and was glad to have Mike occupied with Sam.

I was experienced with modern group sexual events from my experiences at Hillbilly Hollow and also with a Central American Tribe. I had been to several orgy-like events and a bath in Amsterdam and could define the similarities between them and the Rapture activities.

"There was a real sense of brotherhood in the Indian tribe and at Hillbilly Hollow. In both cases most of the participants were related and male sex was an initiation and a mark of adulthood for the males," I explained. "It seemed to be a means of population control for each group too. Man to man sex didn't have the problems heterosexual sex does. It provided an opportunity for men to release their sexual tensions without killing off the women in childbirth."

"That's much the same origins of the Rapture Grange meetings," Bill said. "The men weren't all so closely related, but in a small farming community in the later 19th century, intermarriage could be a problem."

"At Hillbilly Hollow, sex was defined as being between men and woman only. To be sex, it had possibly to result in pregnancy. By definition man to man intercourse wasn't sex." I explained. "In the same way, I studied an Australian tribe which defined nudity by having an exposed cock head. They didn't practice circumcision and as long as the foreskin covered the glans, you were fully dressed."

"It was odd, one of my colleagues was cut and the aborigines found that both shocking and titillating," I explained. "To expose yourself that way was a sign of intimacy and friendship. They didn't know what to make of it."

"How close was the sexual contact between relations?" Tony asked. "It seems they disobeyed all the rules about incest."

"Remember it wasn't sex unless it involved woman. It wasn't sex; it was messing around. The closeness varied. In the Indian tribe, man seed was the source of strength and you wanted to make sure your sons got yours as well as the seed of the strongest and most powerful men of the tribe." I said.

"How did they take it?" Tony asked.

"After some drinking and ceremonial dancing, the seed went straight from the cock into the deepest part of the ass," I replied. "I think the father's cock was supposed to be the first to enter, but I had a feeling, most of the guys cheated a little with their older brothers and cousins. It was older men fucking the younger men at first. As the ritual progressed and everyone got drunker, it was wide open."

"Now, Hillbilly Hollow, it was an Uncle, or older cousin who fucked you first. Sex play with your father was later and entirely voluntary. It wasn't required," I said. "As far as I could tell, everyone did eventually. It was a male bonding event, but there may have been other explanations."

"Such as?" Bill asked.

"The Wilson's always claimed they were inbred and they kept on getting hornier as they kept on screwing their sisters," I said. "All of them seemed to have well developed sex drives. Quite frankly, they never were that picky when it came to selecting partners, except mothers and sisters were strictly off limits."

Sam, Tony, Mike, Bill and I were sitting in the hot tub when Virgil appeared. He came to check out the two new men. Mike and Tony passed with flying colors. Tony's Italian good looks impressed him. His cock was thick and uncut, a classic Italian sausage.

Nude Mike was a surprise. He was very muscular and toned; he wasn't a muscle man, but he was in great shape. He was also just about the whitest man I had ever seen. He was pale, but healthy, with pearly skin with pink highlights. His chest was hairy, but the hair was fine and white so it all but disappeared. Mike's cock was long, thin and cut. Mike was still talking to Sam when Virgil joined us. Virgil knew a lot more about the Grateful Dead than any sensible man should. Virgil and Mike hit it off too.

I noticed Virgil was hard when he got in the tub. That didn't seem to bother Mike at all. Virgil sat on the edge of the tub with his erection in view. Mike wasn't as hard as Virgil, but he was a long way from being soft. Mike had evidently made peace with being naked in a bunch of guys.

Tony was much taken with Bill's monster cock. Like me, he hadn't guessed Bill was so well endowed. We talked well into the night and although the evening was filled with the anticipation of sex, we went to bed with no activity of a sexual nature. I wondered if that would effect the next day's activities.

Lou and Mitch came over for breakfast the next morning. Mitch took me aside. "You will play with Lou? He has his heart set on it," he asked.

"Sure I enjoyed our time at the last meeting. I enjoyed my time with you too," I said. Mitch blushed. He was unaccustomed to praise of any sort.

"Lou has a friend from the Rehab Center he wants you to meet," Mitch continued. "Lou can hardly talk. You can't believe how good it has been for him to be trying so hard. I mean, it's not easy to figure out want he's trying to say, but after years he is trying."

"Don't worry. I'll do my part," I said. We went off the Grange Hall. This time I entered on the other side, and Tony and Mike went to the new comer's door. The Johnson brothers were waiting for me. We went to the meeting room and there were a few men standing around. After a few minutes, Mitch and Lou arrived with a third man. I assumed he was Lou's friend. They walked over to me.

"Gus, this is Martin." Mitch said. I shook hands. Martin was a good-looking kid of maybe 23-25. He had dark brown hair and a small mustache. He combed his hair to hide a gash on one side of his head. One arm and leg were shrunken. I could see the effect of the head injury.

"Grizzly!" Martin cried. He hugged me. I realized what had happened. I don't know if Lou thought I was Grizzly Adams, or if I just looked like him. Whatever he thought, I hit the spot for him and his friend. When Martin hugged me, he ran his hands over my furry back. Martin almost melted.

This had happened once or twice before, when I had run into men who were really turned on by fur. Martin just held me and patted my back and cradled his head on my chest. He also was getting hard and rubbing his cock against me. Lou cuddled up on the other side and we formed a tight cluster. Mitch was looked at us as if he was a matchmaker who had just made the particularly good match.

For me, cuddling turns into something more overtly sexual. I didn't know if it affected these men the same way. Martin's cock answered the question for me. It would be more correct to say his cock and his mouth responded. He slipped to the floor and began nursing my cock. We moved over to a bench against the wall. I was able to suck Lou while Martin sucked delicately on my cock. His movements could be jerky and I think he was afraid he might hurt me. After a while Lou and Martin traded places. Martin must not have expected me to suck him. He first looked shocked and then he began to glow.

He didn't last long. He turned ridged as a stone; then he filled my mouth with his ball cream. I held him tight and took the whole load. It was a young man's load and I was pretty sure it was a good week's supply. He calmed down and I sucked Lou again with the same results. Both men looked pleased and almost serene as they came down from their sexual high. Mitch looked after them like a mother lion, protecting his den.

"It will take them a while to recover," he whispered. "Go and play some. Do you think you could come back later?" I said, sure. Bill was waving at me from a corner of the room. I went over to see what he wanted.

Chapter 6

I walked over to Bill. I noticed Mike was with Virgil. Virgil sucked him while he sucked another man I didn't know. Tony was talking to one of the Johnson brothers. Bill waved at Tony to come over too.

"This is wild," Tony said. "I really didn't believe what you said was true." There were 20 to 25 men in the room now, all connected genitally to one or two others, either sucking or fondling. Anal activity hadn't started yet. "Five or six guys have sucked me already," Tony said; he was at half-staff. "It's a really friendly group!"

"Those were just greeting sucks, if your cock is any indication," Bill said. "Most like to hold off on the orgasm producing sex until later. "

"They certainly were getting me revved up," Tony said.

"Well, if you're ready to move on to something more intense, I've got a friend who'd like to meet you two." Jim said, "Let me take you into my parlor and you can look at my collection of etchings." We went behind a partition wall and a section of paneling opened to reveal a hidden door.

We walked into the next room. It was small, but had a mirrored ceiling and walls. There was a leather ottoman, the size of a couch and a sling hanging from the ceiling. There were two men in the room. One was short and stocky, the other tall and muscular.

"Gus, Tony, I'd like you to meet Bob and Franklin," Bill said. Bob was the short one. He was in his early sixties, distinguished looking, with gray hair, bushy eyebrows and a broad smile. He was a hairball, but looked solid rather than dumpy. His uncut cock and balls were massive too. His cock was relaxed, drooping over his tangerine sized balls. He cock formed a 5" tube, squared off at the end by his foreskin. His balls were the size of tangerines.

Franklin was physically the opposite of Bob. He was a good six feet, muscular and toned. He had a flat top, and shaved his tanned body except to a square of hair at his pubes. While Bob smiled and seemed friendly, Franklin stood back. I realized he was a State Trooper, and Bob was a high-ranking judge indeed. While Franklin was standoffish, his cock was hard and there was a bead of pre cum glistening in the slit. He was more interested than his face indicated.

Bob came over to me and we talked. He had an impressive, deep voice. "You teach with Bill?"

"Yes, we're in the same department. We also seem to share the same interests, but I didn't know that until a month or two ago," I replied. "I also didn't know he was hung like Trigger."

Bob laughed. "That's what I knew about him first!" he said. "Virgil knows my interests and when he ran into Jim, he got me to come to the next meeting. Just for scientific interests, you know." I smiled at him; we understood each other.

"I like them big, but it's not an obsession," I said.

"To tell you the truth, it is an obsession for me," Bob said. "You'd think it would be the sort of thing you outgrow, but it just got stronger in me as I aged. Part of the problem was I didn't act on it at all. I just pretended it wasn't there and caught a rare glimpse from time to time. You've got a nice one, too."

"I tend to like masculine, hairy men," I said. "I have been acting on my desires. I'm not too sure you can do much about fetishes or obsessions. I don't know where they come from, but they seem to be hard wired into you psychological makeup. As long as they don't hurt anyone, why worry?"

"You're a college professor; I'm a judge. It seems undignified to be chasing after cocks," Bob said. He was weighing my balls with his hands, so I figured he had succumbed to the temptation.

"Somehow we've gotten ourselves into the position of thinking that your status or profession in life divorces you from human drives and emotions. That, combined with the effort to make sex into a sinful exercise, leaves you trapped between a rock and a hard cock," I remarked. "Let face it, there are a lot of people who will only be satisfied if you are a monk."

"I think you are right about that," Bob said. He dropped to his knees and began sucking me, ending the conversation. Tony was nursing Franklin's cock. Franklin almost looked relaxed. Bob and I relocated to the large ottoman. I was on my back, while Bob sucked my cock. Bill straddled my head and dangled his cock in my face. I opened my mouth and his cock dripped some pre cum.

Bob worked on my cock, then balls. He worked his way to my ass and rimmed me. He was good at it too. He fingered my ass when he wasn't trying to get his tongue into my ass. I don't mind being rimmed but being fucked is better. Bob must have been able to read my thoughts.

Soon my legs were on Bob's shoulders and his cock was at my hole. He pushed and I soon realized Bob was thick. I hadn't seen him get hard, but it felt as if he was trying to force a fire plug into my ass. Bill noticed I was having a problem and produced a bottle of poppers and gave me a good sniff. They did the trick.

Bill moved and got behind Bob. Bob bent over me and I realized Bill was going to fuck Bob. Bob's thick meat was fully lodged in my ass, when Jim rammed Bob. Bill thrust so hard I felt it, transmitted deep into my ass by Bob's cock. I was being double fucked by both men. I could feel Bob's excitement as he was genitally linked to two men. Bob couldn't last long wedged between my tight ass' stimulation of his cock and Jim's cock's stimulation of his ass. Bob was moaning as he shot off. He pulled out and sprayed me with his seed.

Bill pulled out and let Bob cool off. "Are you okay, Bob?" he asked.

"Okay isn't the word for it," Bob said. "How are you Gus? You were great."

I got off the ottoman. I looked down at my body. It looked as if it had been glazed by Bob's cum. Bob's cock had shrunk some since his orgasm, but it still did look like a fire-plug.

"I'm fine. Messy, but fine," I said. Franklin walked over to me and began licking sperm off my chest. There was nothing cool and collected about Franklin as he did this. He gave every indication be being a confirmed cum hound. I lay back on the ottoman to let him lick it all up. This time Tony straddled me so I could suck his cock.

Franklin was really into cum, and by the time he was done, no trace of Bob's man seed was left on my body. Tony later told me, Franklin wasn't into cock; he wanted cum. He would suck to get the sperm out of the balls. Tony, Bill and I went back into the main room. Bob had to get back to the state capital for an evening meeting.

There were a good forty men going at it as we rejoined the group. Tony went off to see how Mike was doing. Mike was with Robert, the older man we had met at the first meeting who looked like Santa Claus. Robert was on his back and Mike's cock was slowly pumping the older man's ass as they had a rather spirited conversation. Tony joined them. The next time I looked, it was Tony's cock in Robert's ass. All was well there.

Lou and Mike were playing with the Johnson brothers. Clearly once Lou got the hang of it, he was on automatic pilot. The Johnsons were nice men and it looked as if the foursome was sexually compatible.

Mitch came over to me. "They are two happy guys," he said, shaking my hand. "You were everything they wanted."

"I'm glad to help, but I didn't do anything, other than let my cock do the thinking for me," I said.

"I talked to one of the Therapists at Rehab," Mitch continued. "He said that men in their situation with the damage they have sustained feel broken and undesirable. They tend to think pity is the only thing that could possibly attract anyone. The therapist told me in a roundabout way, if they could feel sexually desirable again, it would help a lot. You did that for them." Mitch was on the verge of getting teary again.

A man I didn't know came over. "Hi, Mitch!" he called in a booming voice, "Who's the stud muffin?"

"This is Gus, a friend from out of town," Mitch said. "Gus, this is Edward Ballard. He's warden at the local home for bad boys." We shook hands. Edward was average in height, compact and beefy, with his black hair crew cut and well-trimmed mustache. I guessed he worked out, since the beef was solid. He was mostly smooth except for a thick pubic bush. His cut cock head just barely poked out of the forest.

"I hope everyone has been making you feel welcome," Edward said. "Mitch here is a good guy." He put his arm around Mitch's shoulder. "A real good guy," he added, as he rubbed the fur on Mitch's back. There was something about the way he said it that let me know Edward was more than casually interested in Mitch. I glanced down and saw Edward's cock poke further out of the bush.

"Everyone has made me feel really welcome. I was here a few months ago and liked it so much, I decided to come back," I said. "Everyone is so friendly." As I said that, I dropped to my knees and licked Edward's cock head. I reached up and got Mitch's cock and then pulled him closer, so I could suck both cocks.

Edward had a lollipop style cock, with a half dollar sized mushroom on a long, thin, curving shaft. He had showered just before he came to the meeting and he tasted of soap. Mitch's cock was thick, stubby and uncut. He had been fermenting a brew of pre cum and man spunk inside the skin. I got the two cocks close enough and, since Mitch wasn't fully hard, I docked Edward's cock in Mitch's foreskin.

I don't think of myself as a mind reader, but I sure found Edward's on button. He started kissing Mitch, as I stroked Mitch's foreskin over Edward's cock. There was more than enough skin, and even after Mitch got hard, there was still some left over for Edward. Mitch motioned for me to get up. When I did, he dropped to his knees and sucked Edward and me.

"You like this, don't you?" I whispered to him as Mitch sucked us.

"Shit yes, fucking hot!"

"Are you a sucker or a fucker?" I asked.

"Sucker, love to 69 and top," he whispered. "I bottom for the right guy," he added, as he dropped is voice a bit lower. I knew he wanted to have sex with me and the offer to bottom was his insurance policy. He didn't want to lose out on the sex, if I was a pure top.

"Are you being polite or do you want a cock in your ass," I asked.

Edward smiled. "I was being polite and yes I want it in my ass bad," he replied. I got Mitch up from the floor.

"Edward and I are interested in a little fuck fest. Are you game?" Mitch nodded. "Are you full service, or top only?"

"Versatile," he answered. "You are too, aren't you?"

"I sure am, so is Edward," I added.

"Edward is a top." Mitch said.

"Not today," I said.

"Who goes first?" Edward asked.

"Let's all lube up our cocks and asses and see what develops," I suggested. One of the nice things about the Grange meeting is that sex is required and unashamed. No one seemed to notice or care when three men started to lubricate their cocks and bend over and open their asses wide so a friend could lubricate the fuck hole. I poked a few fingers into Edward's ass and found his prostate.

I pressed the small gland and Edward moaned. That was a good sign. I pressed harder and his knees almost buckled. That was an even better sign. He may not have bottomed much, but the raw materials for being a bottom were there. Everything that could feel in his ass was there and in working condition. A man I didn't know walked by and whispered, "Lube him up good, he loves it when he's turned on." As I said, it was a friendly group.

Mitch lubricated my ass. I told him I wanted to take his cock. He wanted me to take Edward's first. "It'll open you up some," he said. Edward was more than willing. I got on my back, and he hoisted my legs on his shoulders and positioned his mushroom at my hole.

"Are you ready?" he asked. I said yes and he pushed the head through the sphincter and then rested his cock head just inside the ass ring. "Okay?" Edward asked. I nodded and he pushed the rest of his dick deep into my ass.

It was good. Most cocks have a knob on a shaft, but Edward's cock head was so big it seemed to be almost detached as I felt it travel the length of my love chute. His shaft was so thin, I could barely feel it.

Edward leaned forward. "Are you ready for Mitch's cock?" he asked. We were both enjoying it, but I guessed Mitch was going to be the main attraction for him. Edward didn't want to shoot off too early.

"Let's give Mitch's fire plug cock a trial run," I said. Edward pulled out. Mitch was always holding back some, but I got up and got him to get on the bench so I should sit on it. Mitch's cock was shorter than Bill or Red's meat, but just as thick. By sitting on it, I had some control and could set the pace.

Mitch's was rock hard so I knew he was ready. I straddled him and slowly lowered myself on his cock. His cock head was easy; the shaft was another matter all together. He was two or three inches in when I realized he was a bit thicker than the men who had fucked me at the last meeting.

By wiggling my hips, I was able to lower myself on the cock. It wasn't fast, but by the time my hip rested on his pelvis, all was well. It was a snug fit, but I liked it and Mitch was almost crying it felt so good. I was massaging his cock with my ass, masturbating him with my sphincter. I continued to undulate my hips and his cock got more and more comfortable and exciting.

"Lean forward some," Edward asked; I did. He had spread Mitch's legs and was now sucking the bear-like man's bull balls. I raised myself so that only Mitch's cock-head remained in my ass. Before I had a chance to sit back on it again, Edward was there, licking the exposed shaft of Mitch's cock. As I leaned backward; the cock slipped at a different angle and made a direct hit on my prostate.

Suddenly my entire weight was concentrated on my prostate, balanced in Mitch's rock hard fire-plug. It was as intense a sexual feeling as I had ever experienced. I don't know exactly what happened next. I was pretty much out of it, but Lou and Martin reappeared. I know I shot off, and got off Mitch's cock as I shot. He popped too, spraying my ass with his seed. Martin cleaned up my cum which had sprayed all over my hairy chest. Lou ate Mitch's cum, trying to get his tongue deep into my ass. He didn't want to miss any of his friend's seed.

All good things come to an end. The party ended and we returned to Sam's. I expected to return to Rapture Grange soon, but events intervened. A close friend died. He was set to lead a major expedition to Central America that summer. I was asked to take his place. I agreed and spent the next two years traveling. I thought about the Grange often and hoped I would get a chance to return.

About the Author

Bob Archman is a retired man living in rural Virginia. He has liked mysteries ever since he got his first Hardy Boy's book in 1957. He also likes Agatha Christie's mature detectives, Hercule Poirot and Jane Marple. He is interested in relationships between mature, hard working men. He tends to write about men who are actively engaged in their jobs and life and happen to be gay, rather than gay men who happen to have a job. A friend of his once asked, "Why be gay and not like sex?" Most of the men in Bob Archman's novels know the answer to that question.

www.ingramcontent.com/pod-product-compliance
Lightning Source LLC
Chambersburg PA
CBHW051134260626
47170CB00005B/1802